REPENT

THE SENSITIVES BOOK SIX

RICK WOOD

BLOOD SPLATTER PRESS

ABOUT THE AUTHOR

Rick Wood is a British writer born in Cheltenham.

His love for writing came at an early age, as did his battle with mental health. After defeating his demons, he grew up and became a stand-up comedian, then a drama and English teacher, before giving it all up to become a full-time author.

He now lives in Loughborough, where he divides his time between watching horror, reading horror, and writing horror.

I Do Not Belong

Death of the Honeymoon

Sean Mallon:

Book One – The Art of Murder

Book Two – Redemption of the Hopeless

The Edward King Series:

Book One – I Have the Sight

Book Two – Descendant of Hell

Book Three – An Exorcist Possessed

Book Four – Blood of Hope

Book Five – The World Ends Tonight

Non-Fiction

How to Write an Awesome Novel

Thrillers published as Ed Grace:

The Jay Sullivan Thriller Series

Assassin Down

Kill Them Quickly

THIS STORY STARTS THREE DAYS
AFTER THE CONCLUSION OF
QUESTIONS FOR THE DEVIL.

LITTLE BENNY HATED BEING CALLED LITTLE BENNY.

He was little, but that was only because he was a child.

After all, what child wasn't little?

None.

Yet you don't see every other nine-year-old in the country being called little by their patronising family. His sister wasn't so bad; sometimes she understood, although she was often stroppy, as he was repeatedly told teenagers were – but his parents were infuriating. They wouldn't stop.

"Little Benny, would you come for tea?"

"Little Benny, time for school!"

"Little Benny, it's time for you bath."

He was nine, after all. Not two. He could bathe by himself. He didn't need his parents there.

It was ridiculous.

So ridiculous.

He lifted his head from the well-padded pillow. Looked around his room. Shadows covered darkness. His Kylo Ren action figure remained on the floor next to Rey, the curtains remained untwitched, and the shadows on his dinosaur wall-paper didn't flicker.

I know you can hear me.

He closed his eyes.

It was late. He was exhausted. He'd remained awake in protest, but no one knew. Why would they? Why would anyone care enough to go check whether Little Benny was asleep?

I'm here with you...

He ignored it again. It had been persistent over the last few weeks, constantly saying stuff in a hushed whisper, like someone standing by his ear and feeding words into his brain. Sometimes he could feel the brush of breath against his cheek as it whispered, but he knew enough to know nobody was there.

Whatever it was, it would just go away eventually.

That's what Thea had said when he'd told her.

"It's just your imagination being overactive; it'll go, don't worry," she had said.

He didn't tell his parents. Not his annoying parents who called him Little Benny.

But he'd told his sister. His sister who always understood.

Thea. His hero. His best friend.

With his sister as his final thought, his mind left this world and found its way into his subconscious. He dreamt about going to the toy shop his parents sometimes took him to, but when he arrived, all the toys had sold out. All, apart from one. One little toy.

A creepy little toy.

A toy that stared at him.

That smiled.

Like a clown, but not. The body of an action figure. The puffiness of a stuffed bear. Like the flawed aspects of numerous toys morphed into one.

And it laughed.

Slowly, low-pitched, and drawn-out.

Heh. Heh. Heh. Heh.

"Why are you laughing?" Ben asked.

Its laughing ceased, but its smirk remained. It tilted its head to the side, slanting peculiarly, as if inspecting Ben. As if in the middle of a twisted thought.

"What is it?" Ben asked.

Its tilting stopped. Its head stayed stuck in its position, but its grin seemed to widen – even though the grin didn't move, it looked like it grew.

"What are you–"

The toy lifted its finger to its lips and gently shushed.

Then it spoke.

Wake up, Ben. It's time.

His eyes opened. Morning light crept between the gap in the curtains. His room came into focus, the shadows far lighter, his messy pile of toys becoming less blurred.

He was sweating.

He sat up and moved his feet to the floor, feeling the tufts of carpet poke between his toes. He paused for a moment, feeling strangely odd, like he was there but not – like his body was his, but belonged to somebody else.

Go downstairs, Ben.

Ben stood, left his room, walked to the stairs, moving with robotic precision, ensuring to place his foot in the same position on each step.

He entered the kitchen and there everyone was. Thea sat at the table, drawing something in her sketch book, like she often did. His dad sat at the table, a coffee in his hand, the *Telegraph* in the other. His mum stood at the stove, cooking some bacon, a perfect Saturday morning breakfast.

"Good morning," his mum said with feigned surprise. "I was

beginning to wonder where you were, you're normally up watching TV before we're awake. Is everything okay?"

Ben paused, then vacantly nodded.

"I was going to go check on you in a moment."

Ben said nothing.

"Well, did you enjoy your lie-in?"

Ben frowned. His lie-in?

What lie-in?

What was she talking about?

What was going on? Where was he? Was he here?

The table, Ben.

He looked to the table. Thea's various shades of pencil were laid out before her – from B7 to H7. Next to that was a rubber and a pencil sharpener.

"You okay, stink-head?" Thea playfully asked, noticing him staring. When Ben's pale face didn't reply, she grew a little perturbed. "Hey, what's going on? Everything okay?"

The pencil sharpener, Ben.

He stepped forward, reached across Thea, and took the pencil sharpener.

"Hey, where are you going with that?" she asked.

He looked at the pencil sharpener. Held it in the palm of his hand, gazing at it, absently consuming it with his eyes. Every piece of its metal exterior, its light weight, its small size.

"Well don't lose it, I need it," she said, realising she wasn't getting a reply, and continued sketching.

No one looked at him. They all resumed their activities, apparently unaltered by his peculiar lack of conscious attendance.

It's because they don't care, Ben.

That must be it.

Must be.

Little Benny wasn't cared about.

Little Benny was just a strange child.

Little Benny was going to die.

Now, Ben.

Ben closed his fingers around the tiny blade within the pencil sharpener. He pulled at it, his fingers stinging from its sharp indent.

He threw the rest of the pencil sharpener back onto the table but kept the miniscule blade.

It landed on Thea's work.

"Hey, what are you doing?"

I won't ask again, Ben.

He pressed the blade against his wrist. It only hurt a little, so he pushed it in further. And further. And further. Until, eventually, blood seeped out.

Then he pushed it in further.

He dragged the blade across his wrist until blood was bubbling over his arm.

"Ben!" Thea shouted. "Ben, what are you doing?"

His dad looked up, not realising what Ben was doing at first, but once he did, he leapt from his chair.

Finish it, Ben.

This blade wasn't enough.

His dad was coming toward him. His dad was going to stop him.

His dad *couldn't* stop him.

Ben *couldn't* let him.

He rushed over to the kitchen side next to his mum. A wooden block of knives sat snuggly beside his mum's frying pan. Despite the commotion of his dad and his sister rushing after him, she didn't even notice.

Which meant she didn't do a thing when Ben withdrew the longest, sharpest knife they had.

Thea and his dad paused. His dad held his hand out, cautiously, calmly.

"Put the knife down, Ben."

Finish it.

"Put the knife down."

I said finish it.

"Ben, put it down."

I said FINISH IT.

Just as his mum looked up and noticed the commotion, Ben slid the blade across his throat, spraying the floral wallpaper with decorations of his blood.

The last thing he heard was his sister screaming.

NOW

2

THERE WERE RUMOURS THAT THE POPE HIMSELF WOULD BE IN attendance, though most thought such rumours were unfounded – the pope never lessened himself to such meetings.

In all honesty, the pope thought such groups were below him. Father Lorenzo Romano was surprised that such meetings were even allowed to occur under the pope's watch – but, even though the pope detested what they did, and the fact that unordained priests such as the Sensitives were given permission to carry out the Church's hidden duties, it seemed as if the pope understood the necessity. So, even though they didn't have his approval, they had his underhanded permission.

Once everyone had settled in, Lorenzo stood before them, looking out at the crowd. A room beneath the Vatican – it seemed appropriate, somehow, that such a meeting was buried beneath. Not that the Vatican didn't know – but they could plead ignorance. One would have assumed the room was a crypt if it weren't for the ten rows of tiered seats and the speaking area at the front.

Lorenzo was a man in his fifties, though you wouldn't

know it for the energy he expended. He did the job least wanted by the Church, but the one most important: covering up the devastation caused by things that people do not need to know the truth about. He'd been doing it a long time, and his sharp yet weary mind was used to the sights he had to see and the issues he had to fix.

He went to speak, but didn't. He hated this. Everything about it was just...*wrong.*

And that was the feeling of the room. That what was happening in the world was a huge mistake and should have been prevented. The four dank walls contained a constant murmuring of rumours, the priests hypothesising what was going to happen now, how little chance they stood, and how much the Sensitives had completely wrecked everything.

Eventually, Lorenzo spoke. He did so without expecting himself to, his mouth just opened and words came out – it was the only way he would be able to address such an on-edge congregation.

"Good morning," he said.

The under-the-breath speech settled, replaced by nervous shuffling of vestments against wooden seats.

"For those of you that don't know me, and I can see that is very few of you," Lorenzo spoke, scanning the crowd, "may I introduce myself? My name is Father Lorenzo Romano. I am the head of the Cleanser of Paranormal Contention group."

"Why isn't the pope here!" someone shouted out. Their heckle was met with murmurs of agreement.

Lorenzo looked down and sighed. This wasn't going to be easy. He was hoping he could just stand there and talk, hoping this could be swift and painless, that he could just open his mouth and allow explanations to come out quickly, leaving him to back away to his own quarters where he could continue attempting to produce a feasible plan.

"The pope sends his apologies," Lorenzo answered. "Unfortunately, he was unable to make it."

"How could he not be here!"

"He needs to know!"

"We need his guidance!"

"Enough!" barked Lorenzo. "*I* am here. *I* am the pope's representative. Unfortunately, the pope is one of cleansing purity, and does not wish to muddy his hands with demons and exorcisms. It is our job to confront the issue, not his."

"Then what about the Sensitives!" another shouted out.

Even stronger murmurs of confirmation met the outburst.

"They caused this!"

"Yeah!"

"So why aren't they here?"

Lorenzo hesitantly looked over his shoulder to the door.

It was a good question.

Why weren't they here?

They had been hastily invited. In fact, Lorenzo had insisted. They had agreed.

So, where were they?

Had they backed out? Decided they couldn't confront the mess they had made? Decided that the fight was so unwinnable they just wouldn't bother?

Or was Lorenzo just a fool to think they would come in the first place?

"I assure you," Lorenzo insisted, "that the Sensitives have been contacted, and they have confirmed their attendance. I assume their flight could be late, or that–"

Hollers of raucous disagreement met his suggestion. Pure outrage objected to the suggestion.

"They're too scared to face us!"

"Cowards!"

"We are screwed!"

Lorenzo sighed once again, this time a bigger, louder, drawn-out sigh. He didn't disagree with anything these people were saying, but he knew it was his job to lead, and to reassure.

Even though it seemed reassurance was futile.

"Gentlemen, we need to trust in the Sensitives."Even stronger objections shouted their anger.

"I know this could be seen as their fault, but without them, we don't stand a chance. We need to–"

The voices grew overwhelming, the volume too strong.

"It is their fault!"

"We don't stand a chance!"

"They will just make it worse!"

"The Sensitives are–" Lorenzo attempted, but the objections just persisted.

Should he wait for the shouts to stop? Because they weren't stopping anytime soon.

Should he talk over them?

Should he leave?

No, he couldn't leave. What message would that give?

"The Sensitives are–" he tried again, but could barely hear himself.

"The Sensitives are crucial to–" he shouted, but the objections were growing stronger, louder, harder to overcome.

He shook his head. It was no use. These people were right.

Where were the Sensitives?

Then, as if answering his thoughts, a thudding came from the door as it opened.

Every person in the room fell silent. Every objection, every shout, every heckle – every voice turned to dumbfounded shock, and every eye turned to the door.

Lorenzo turned also, and, although he resented them, he was relieved to see them.

"Hello," said Oscar. "We apologise for being late."

He entered and took his place at the front, beside Lorenzo, placing a grateful hand on his shoulder.

"Thank you for waiting for us," Oscar said.

Julian and April followed in and stood beside him.

Together, they looked out at the angry, silent faces, all waiting to hear what they had to say.

3

IF HOSTILITY AND ANGER HAD A STENCH, THIS ROOM WOULD stink of it. As soon as Oscar's foot tapped the stone floor, he could feel the silence descending, feel the retinas burning through his face, could practically hear the resentful thoughts.

It was deserved, he supposed.

It was, of course, his fault.

He was the one who was in the wrong.

Except, he did not feel that he was in the wrong. He did not regret his decision.

He had done what he believed was right.

Even if no one else agreed.

He had made the decision to save April instead of the world. And, as fate would have it, the world had paid with an influx of powerful demons – demons that were causing humans to commit the most horrific of acts. Within a year, these demons could quite easily achieve amalgamation incarnation – the process of no longer being a demon sharing a human's body, but instead, removing that human from their body and claiming it for their own; meaning it would be impossible to exorcise them. They would then use these bodies as a vessel to pass from Hell to Earth, leaving them to sit back and watch as the human population devoured itself to extinction.

Yes, he had done what he believed was right – but he had done what everyone else believed was wrong.

Everyone stared at him, waiting for him to speak. He wished he'd prepared what he was going to say a bit more. Then again, what could he say? There was nothing that could undo what was happening. There was nothing that could lessen the overwhelming fight they had. There was nothing that any words could do to increase their lessening chances.

Oscar glanced over his shoulder for reassurance. April's ever-doting eyes stared back at him and she gave him a subtle nod, a gentle push as if to say, *go on, you can do it.*

Julian didn't look at him. His face, displaying an expression of detest, remained focussed elsewhere. Even though Julian had refused to say a word to Oscar in the past two weeks, he'd still managed to convey his unaltering thoughts and feelings about the situation to Oscar with just his facial expression alone.

Oscar looked to Lorenzo. Lorenzo looked back expectantly, prompting Oscar to say something that would somehow make this situation better.

Then he looked back to the crowd before him. Expectant faces – all with raised, expectant eyebrows and grimaced, downturned lips.

"Good morning," Oscar began. "Thank you all for attending today. I think it's of the utmost importance that we have this meeting now, so we can air our grievances, and start to think of a plan forward."

A man began to object, but Oscar lifted a hand that somehow silenced him. This surprised Oscar, though he tried not to show it – he'd never been the kind of person who could easily command a room.

"Please, listen to what we have to say, and then you may speak afterwards."

The man who had begun to object raised a hand out as if to prompt Oscar to go on – but the rigid pointedness of the man's gesture showed that he was already inclined to dislike the following words.

"There is no excuse for what I have done. For what *we* have done."

Oscar didn't need to look at Julian to know he was flinching at the suggestion that this wasn't all just down to Oscar – but April had told Oscar that they needed to be together on this, that the Sensitives needed to take collective responsibility, if only to enforce their own solidarity.

"The most honest thing I can say is probably that we had to face some very difficult choices. Some impossible choices. And some may view the choices that we made as the wrong ones."

"Some may view?" another man shouted out.

"Please, I have asked for silence; you can voice your opinion after I have spoken."

"But what you did was wrong; don't you dare deny it!"

Oscar looked over his shoulder at April. She looked vulnerable, worried for Oscar.

He stepped forward, making eye contact with each and every member of his audience.

"How much do you even know of what I did, huh?" It wasn't *we* anymore – it was now *I*. These people deserved brutal honesty. "Huh? How many of you actually know? Or have you just heard rumours?"

An uncomfortable hush responded. The man shouted out once again.

"Then why don't you tell us?"

"Fine. I had a choice. Save the world or save the woman I love. And I chose the option I saw as right. That I still see as right."

A crescendo of groans spread across the priests.

"Before you object, or start demanding my head, let me ask you this – what do you preach in your sermons? Huh? What do you ask of your congregation? Tell me that."

Oscar took a big, deep breath. He knew how important his next set of words were going to be.

"Love. That's what. You preach love, and you preach that we do what we have to for love, do you not?"

A wave of irritable moans replied.

"Let me ask you a question – if we don't do things for love, if we don't do things with those we care about in the forefront of our minds – then what are we fighting for? What is the point?"

"Rubbish!" came the first response, which prompted the next.

"Shut up!"

"Nonsense!"

The first man who'd objected stood up.

"We preach such messages to ordinary people. People whose actions don't risk everything!"

"I am an ordinary–"

"You are a *Sensitive*! You are above this! You are supposed to be the ones who sacrifice love so others can put it first!"

Oscar realised he was holding his breath, and he let it go.

He'd failed them.

He had no way to tell them otherwise.

And his response had fallen short. These people were not ready to forgive him.

"You did this!"

"Get out!"

"Just leave!"

People stood, people shouted, threw their arms in the air, voiced their enraged objections. The volume grew and the walls closed in until Oscar felt like he was trapped in a box of noise.

He looked to April and Julian. They had nothing.

Lorenzo appeared at Oscar's side.

"I think it's time we left these people to it, don't you think?"

Oscar tamely nodded.

"This way," Lorenzo said, leading Oscar out of the room, followed by Julian and April.

They could hear the shouts all the way down the corridor.

4

EVEN THOUGH THEA WAS SURROUNDED BY PEOPLE, SHE STOOD alone. Even though her mum and dad were either side of her, it meant nothing. Her little brother was gone.

A nine-year-old boy who dreamt of becoming an archaeologist. A nine-year-old boy who followed her around everywhere she went and insisted on doing everything she did. A nine-year-old boy who was the sweetest, most lovely brother she could ever have asked for.

She was six when he had been born, and she remembered it like it had just happened. Her dad collected her from school and told her that she had a baby brother. He'd said, "We're going to call him Ben, is that okay with you?" As if he wanted her to be involved, as if she was part of the decision.

She'd answered, "Yes, of course." She often wondered what would have happened if she had said no.

This was the same church where he was christened. She'd remembered the day, remembered feeling annoyed she hadn't had as much attention, and her uncle had spent ages talking to her before telling her that he thought she was going to be a "brilliant older sister."

And she had always tried to be.

But now there was no more being a brilliant older sister. No more surprising him at the school gates that she was picking him up instead of their parents, taking him to the sweet shop with her pocket money, singing their favourite songs on the walk home.

No more drawings he did for her that always spelt her name f-e-a-r.

No more holding hands in the car when he fell asleep.

Instead, she was surrounded by people who knew Ben, but most of whom she didn't even recognise. A vicar stood at the front, saying kind words about a boy he didn't even know. As if it meant anything to him.

Outside, the press. Wanting photos of the funeral of one of the most bizarre deaths of recent years. A nine-year-old committing suicide in front of his family. A tragic death of a child, and the sodding paparazzi decide to hound a grieving family for a gimmick, for a newspaper article that someone could talk about over the water cooler at work.

She wondered how much a picture of her crying would be worth to the *Daily Mail*.

And now they stood, the curtain drawn around a coffin that was too small. The curtain billowed, pushing out as the flames surrounded the boy inside them. She wasn't planning on crying. She was planning on doing it all alone in her bedroom later – but she couldn't help it. She just kept thinking about how it was her little brother in there, being burnt to death.

He didn't kill himself.

Yes, he sliced his own throat – but Thea wouldn't believe it. Wouldn't accept it.

Why would Ben kill himself?

A nine-year-old boy doesn't think of suicide. Especially not a nine-year-old boy with such a zest for life.

Then she felt it. That familiar feeling she'd fought all her life. That feeling like someone was here that shouldn't be here.

That something was watching her.

Thea.

She looked over her shoulder, as if she could hear his voice. As if she could sense him, like he was calling her.

She saw him.

Standing between the pews of the church, in the aisle brides so often walk down. He looked at her and smiled. He waved. He was wearing his stormtrooper costume – his favourite costume.

She waved back at him.

This may seem like a strange occurrence, but to her, it wasn't. Things like this happened all the time. She often saw people others couldn't see – but she knew well enough to know it wasn't normal, and that to say it aloud would see her getting sectioned.

He turned and walked away.

At least he got to say goodbye.

She looked up, directing her stare to a row of people further back. A person was looking at her. A woman, in her twenties, wearing a black dress. Staring. Gormless. Empty, hollow, vengeful stares.

The woman's face morphed into blackness. Her teeth wriggled with worms, her eyes glowed red, her skin faded to a deathly grey.

This wasn't anything abnormal, either. This often happened to people when she looked at them. Then she'd read about the person in the paper a few days later, and find out they were in some kind of horrific event.

Only, she seemed to be seeing these things more often since Ben's death. Like something had changed in the past few weeks.

It still scared her. Still made her worry. But she did what

she always did – she turned away and told herself it was nothing.

The vicar was staring at her.

Just the same as the woman.

His mouth opened, baring his teeth, gangrenous and decayed, black gunk stuck to his gums. His hands grew, his nails turning yellow, sharp, growing around the altar.

She wished she could unsee it, but she couldn't.

She looked away, but he snapped at her, moving his jaw like a dilapidated crocodile. He wanted her attention. He was insisting on it.

She just wanted to grieve for her brother.

She looked over her shoulder. No one else seemed to be seeing this. Same as always, it was just her. An immortally sinister vision burning into her mind.

His eyes grew, bursting from their sockets, expanding, fangs curving from his mouth.

She closed her eyes and dropped her head.

Please, she thought. *Please stop. Please just leave me alone.*

She detested seeing these things.

And she didn't like that she knew it was real. That it wasn't psychosis.

Then again, isn't that what someone with psychosis would say?

No, because she could smell it. The crusted mould of his fingers, the scraping shuffle of scaled legs, the burning of the cross around his neck scalding his chest.

She opened her eyes.

The smell had gone.

The vicar was stood, normally, looking like a human, his hands together and his head face down.

She cried, and not just for her brother.

She looked back at the curtain, still billowing, still cremating her favourite person in the world.

She could feel breath on the back of her throat.
Hissing of a vile image waiting for her to turn around.
She didn't turn around.
She just focussed on her brother.
Her nine-year-old brother, who had taken his own life.
Her nine-year-old brother, who was being cremated.

5

No one spoke as they shuffled into the dank cellar of a room. Lorenzo held the door open for Oscar, followed by Julian and April. There was a table ready for them to sit at, but no one used it – they all stood idly, looking everywhere but at each other.

"Well," Oscar said, unable to bear the silence any longer. "That could have gone better."

"What did you expect?" asked Lorenzo.

Oscar went to answer, then didn't. What had he expected? A room full of understanding faces?

No. In all honesty, that went pretty much as it should have done.

"Why don't we take a seat?" suggested Lorenzo, indicating the table.

Julian sat first, folding his arms, looking away from Oscar with the same sneer painted on his face. Oscar and April gave each other a smile and a small squeeze of each other's hands as they took their seats, followed by Lorenzo.

Everything about the room felt like it was centuries old. The wooden table splintered into Oscar's arms as he leant on it, and the wooden chair was so hard he could feel the bones of his buttocks growing sore against it. This was a church, but it was not still the 1880s, right?

"So, what are your thoughts?" Oscar directed at Lorenzo.

Lorenzo snorted an ironic laugh.

"What?" Oscar inquired.

"What are my thoughts?" Lorenzo repeated. "You know who I am, right? What I do?"

Oscar felt Julian's judgemental eyes on him, so he met them, and they instantly turned away.

"The Cleanser of Paranormal Contention," Oscar confirmed.

"Yes, I know you know my title. But do you actually know what it involves?"

Oscar shrugged. "To some extent."

"Every screw-up you've ever had, I'm the one who has to swoop in and clean it up. I'm the one who has to disguise it so the fragile human population can't know the hard truth about what lurks above and below us."

"But every mess that we create is justifiable–"

"I'm glad you described it as a mess, Oscar, because that is what it is. And I'm tired of cleaning it all up."

Lorenzo looked to April and Julian.

"That goes for all of you," Lorenzo bluntly stated.

"I'm sure the mess became greater when Oscar came along," Julian muttered, prompting Oscar to roll his eyes.

"For the love of God, pull yourselves together," Lorenzo objected, shaking his head at the torn group sat petulantly before him. "And for your information, no, Julian, things did not increase when Oscar was introduced. In fact, things were worse when Derek was at the helm. After the Edward King war, after multiple demons came from holes in the ground, after their battle left an entire field and playground in hellish disarray, I thought that would be the pinnacle of it. And when

Derek died, I thought maybe my job wouldn't be so strenuous."

"Everything Derek did–" Julian tried to interject, but didn't get very far.

"But no, I'm still having to deal with your shit. The body of a man and a toddler in a lake. A deserted prison left to ruins. And now, this – the biggest demonic attack the world has faced since the 1940s. Do you have any idea of the devastation this will bring? The wars this demonic influence will bring about? The genocide? The massacres?"

Oscar and April looked uncomfortably at each other, like they deserved the rant – but Lorenzo wasn't done.

"No. Because love was involved; so who cares if you have prompted the death of millions, or even billions, or probably the entire human race? Who cares if you have given way to Hell to reclaim their place on this Earth? Because you did it for *love*."

Lorenzo glared at each of them in turn, but none of them met his stare.

"Yes. That's right. You truly have fucked this up now."

Julian huffed and sat up.

"As much as I agree with you," Julian said, "and as much as I love to see it pointed out to…" He wouldn't even say Oscar's name. "This is not productive. We're wasting time."

Lorenzo scoffed.

"We're wasting time?" Lorenzo retorted, as if the impudence of the suggestion was the most offensive thing he'd ever heard.

"Yes, we are. We're aware of what's been done and what the consequences are. But sitting around listening to you rant is not progress. If we are going to fight, we need to get on with it."

Oscar felt ashamedly grateful to Julian for ending Lorenzo's rant, even though he knew Julian wasn't doing it for his sake.

"Okay then," Lorenzo sat, waving a hand in the air as he sat back defiantly. "What do you plan, then?"

"Well, we have two lines of enquiry," Oscar said, regretting referring to their plan as 'lines of enquiry,' aware of how much he sounded like a defensive politician. "Julian?"

"Yes," Julian replied. "I have a theory. Something in Derek's journals. But I don't wish to share it until I can confirm more."

They all looked to Julian, as if waiting for him to elaborate, but no further explanation came.

"Well that's helpful, isn't it?" Lorenzo shook his head and rolled his eyes. Julian didn't care.

"Well, our main focus, while Julian does that," Oscar said, "is to search for more like us. More Sensitives. There has to be more out there."

"And you suppose to find them...where?"

"Well – that's still something we're working on, but it is our intention to–"

"It is your *intention*? And, tell me, Oscar – what do you plan to do with these Sensitives you will so inevitably find?"

"We prepare them for war."

Lorenzo stared blankly back at Oscar.

"And how do you plan to do that?"

"Father Romano," April said. "I appreciate that you are sceptical, but Oscar is doing all he can, and your attitude isn't productive. We are doing our best."

Oscar flinched at the words *we are doing our best*. He appreciated what April was doing, but he knew the irritation such a sentence would prompt, considering the cause of the mess.

"Well, luckily for you," Lorenzo said, "we have already had this idea of yours, and we have begun a search ourselves."

"You mean, you are looking for more Sensitives?"

"We *have* been looking for Sensitives, yes. And we've found some."

"You found some?"

"Yes. A boy and a girl. The boy, Sebastian, twenty-one years old, appears to be an adept exorcist. And the girl, still a teenager, sixteen I think, Madison, is a gifted conduit."

Oscar exchanged a surprised look with April, then attempted to exchange one with Julian, who still didn't return his gaze.

"I suggest that you concentrate on training them, and we will concentrate on recruiting more. Once we have found them, we will send them your way. That is, if you feel you can do this without messing it up."

"I'm sure we can manage it."

Lorenzo stood. The others followed.

"Then I think we're done here," Lorenzo decided. "The Sensitives will go home with you. Get them ready – immediately. I have a feeling this war has already begun, and we are already late to it."

"We will. I promise, we won't let you down."

Lorenzo glared at Oscar, evidently unappreciative of the sentiment.

"I wouldn't make such promises. You never know when love might pop up again."

Lorenzo left the room without showing the Sensitives a way out, leaving them to shuffle out on their own.

THEN

6

UNIVERSITY APPEARED TO BE THE OBVIOUS PATH FOR ANY CHILD of a middle-class background, even if it's not always the desired one. It seemed like an expectation, one that the parents bestow on the child before they are truly able to make up their mind for themselves.

Julian resented that his parents had conned him into it.

As much as he liked literature, he didn't want to become an academic in it. He didn't want to sit in a lecture hall debating the metaphor of the moors in *Wuthering Heights*. He didn't want to read into the reason to there being iambic pentameter or no iambic pentameter in a verse of Shakespearean prose. And, most of all, he didn't want to debate what was meant by a particular word used by Chaucer.

This wasn't just because he disliked the course – this was also because he did not enjoy these books. He often wondered how many people that entered an English Literature degree actually read Chaucer or eighteenth-century literature. He loved books because of Lee Child, because of Dan Brown, because of Ira Levin – not because of some outdated book that he couldn't imagine many other eighteen-year-olds reading.

Why couldn't they analyse a book he actually cared about for once?

"And, if you really consider what Sophocles was trying to show by Antigone's relationship to Oedipus was…" the lecturer droned on.

Now they were looking at a play written in 442 BC. It seemed as if they just went hundreds of years further back in time with each morning.

He looked either side of him. He noticed another student who had slated *The Da Vinci Code*, Julian's favourite book – saying that it had an enthralling storyline, brilliant ideas, and great character, but lacked in its use of metaphorical language. He hated her so much. He loved that book because it was entertaining, yet that was never enough for these people.

He'd had enough. He stood and shuffled out, pushed past the legs of ignorant students barely shifting for him to leave.

Just as he reached the door, he heard that voice again, that voice that kept constantly calling his name. Something hushed, distant.

Julian…

He looked over his shoulder.

There it was. Sitting in the place of the girl that he hated. Decrepit. Sinister. A lecherous grin pointed in his direction.

He blinked and it was gone.

Why did he keep seeing these things?

He left, not looking back. Charging out of the door and into the corridor.

"Not for you?" came a voice, the kind of voice that sounded knowledgeable, sounded like it knew stuff. Julian assumed the voice wasn't talking to him.

"Hey, I'm speaking to you," the voice repeated.

Julian turned. Sure enough, there was a man there, looking at him. Julian recognised him as another lecturer in the university, but one that worked in a different department – he couldn't remember the name, but it was one that other students often mocked.

His entitled, over-privileged peers seemed to mock anything that didn't reach their standards.

"I said, is English Literature not for you?"

"I guess not," Julian replied, looking peculiarly at this man, then turned to leave.

"Maybe you should think about changing course," the man spoke again, prompting Julian to stop once more.

"What?"

"My name is Derek Lansdale," the man explained. "I work in the parapsychology and paranormal studies department."

"Paranormal studies?" That was it. The department other students constantly made fun of. The only department more ridiculous than the one slating *The Da Vinci Code*.

"Yes."

"I think I'm good," Julian said, in disbelief at this guy's suggestion. "Thanks, though," he added sarcastically.

"I really think you ought to give it a go."

He kept walking.

"Julian."

He stopped and turned.

"How do you know my name?" Julian demanded.

"Tell me," Derek responded, walking slowly toward him, an air of calm authority in his stride. "Do you ever see things? Feel things? Perhaps notice things about people that they may not be aware of?"

"I said, how do you know my name?"

"There was a girl in there, wasn't there? You could tell something was odd. Something about her seemed strange, didn't it? Evil, maybe?"

"How do you know that?"

Derek reached Julian and placed a firm but reassuring hand on his shoulder.

"Because you have a gift, Julian. I noticed that same girl the other day, and I noticed you noticing her. I could tell that you could tell, too."

"Tell what?"

"That she is possessed."

Julian laughed. "She's not possessed. She's just a bitch."

"Let's get a coffee," Derek suggested. "I'll explain more."

They had the coffee, and Derek did explain more.

Julian changed his course the next day.

Months later, Julian performed his second exorcism, and a child died. He was forced to leave the university, as the course no longer existed due to its primary lecturer being sent to prison.

NOW

7

THE SCHOOL LIBRARY WAS ALWAYS A GOOD PLACE FOR PEOPLE who wanted to seem like they were alone by choice. The truth was, Thea didn't really have anyone to speak to, never mind have lunch with, and she hated other people seeing that. But, if you were alone in the library, it didn't mean that no one liked you – it meant that you were just studying and wanted to concentrate.

In a way, she could convince everyone else almost as much as she could convince herself.

She was convinced, however, that people weren't avoiding her because they necessarily disliked her, and that all of her previous friends hadn't abruptly decided to snub her. It was because no one knew what to say to her.

Her little brother had just killed himself in front of her a little over two weeks ago.

What do you say to someone who's just gone through that?

But, as she placed her History homework on the table in front of her with no intention of doing it, she thought about how it was pretty callous for people's solution to their own awkwardness to be to avoid her. That pretending she didn't exist wasn't the best way to deal with her. For everyone to act like she was a ticking time bomb they couldn't dismantle; that they desperately stayed away from just in case it exploded at any moment – that was not a help.

She stared at the essay question in front of her, her head slumped on her arm, her elbow spread across the table.

SOURCE A OPPOSES *Kaiser Wilhelm II. How do you know?*
Explain your answer using Source A and your contextual knowledge.

[*14 marks*]

NO MATTER how many times she read the question, the words still moulded into a puzzle she couldn't depict.

She didn't even know where Source A was, never mind who this Kaiser guy was and what he wanted.

Who really cared, anyway?

What use would knowing this have to her?

She looked up, deciding to people-watch instead. Curious as to who else was in the library.

Even though the library was relatively full, the tables surrounding hers were still empty. Across the room, a group of girls sat at a table with books out but no intention of studying. They sat around a phone, where Thea assumed one of them was writing a text message, probably to a boy – because when she hit send they all went "oooh" then congratulated each other as if they had just defeated Kaiser Wilhelm II themselves.

If that's a good thing... I still have no idea...

She looked to another table adjacent to the giggling girls, where a couple sat. Again, work was in front of them, but their entwined hands and smacking lips indicated they had no intention of doing it. Someone could come and take the work away and they wouldn't even notice, they were so engrossed in each other's faces. They were getting so fast and their mouths so wide it was as if they were going to eat each other.

Thea wondered if she would ever get to fall in love, and worried that if or when she ever did, someone might try to kiss her like that.

A few tables across from the couple was a boy, sat in the shadow of the corner, between a wall and a book case. Possibly a year seven – one of the youngest in the school. Just two or three years older than Ben. Alone. Reading a kid's book about a girl who joined a bunch of pirates.

The boy looked dorky. His glasses were half the size of his face, his hair was scruffy and unkempt, and his school uniform had clearly been brought for him to grow into.

But something about this boy intrigued her. Caught her intention.

His lips were moving.

At first, Thea assumed his lips were moving in the pattern of the words he was reading. His eyes were eagerly scanning each line.

But the more she stared, the more the words he was mouthing didn't seem to make sense.

She was pretty sure they weren't even English.

"Omn... beak... emin..."

She tried listening more intently, and just about managed to make out the words through his whispers.

"Omnes ibique moriemini... Omnes ibique moriemini..."

What was that?

Latin?

How did a boy like him know Latin?

His face flickered, as if it was a television screen and the signal had briefly gone.

It happened again, and she was sure she could see some kind of visage, some kind of moulded, contorted face appearing on his – but it went so quickly she had no idea what she had actually seen.

His own shadow behind him grew. Stretched. Pulled itself over him.

She was sure she could see a figure in the shadow, but again, couldn't be positive.

"Hey..." she said, trying to get the boy's attention, but he didn't look up.

One of the girls looked at her, sticking her nose up in repulsion.

"Omnes ibique moriemini... Omnes ibique moriemini..."

The shadow grew, the arms of the darkness widening, enveloping the boy in its embrace.

How was no one else seeing this?

"Hey... boy..." she tried again, louder.

The girl turned and stuck her nose up at Thea again. She ignored it.

"Omnes ibique moriemini... Omnes ibique moriemini..."

The shadow came away from the wall, pushing itself to his side, wrapping itself around his body like a father around a child.

"Hey!" she shouted. "Watch out!"

She stood.

The girls fell silent and looked at her.

The couple ceased their make-out session and looked at her.

The boy, alone and unaware, looked up at her.

The shadow continued to stretch itself around the boy, but no one else seemed to be seeing this.

She realised it wasn't real. Well, not to everyone else, anyway.

It was *her* again.

Her sight, or whatever it was.

Hell, maybe she was crazy.

Thea dropped her head, picked up her homework, and scuttled out of the library, ignoring the giggles of the girls as she left.

There were only five minutes left until the bell, so she'd go wait outside her next lesson.

It wouldn't look strange for her to be there on her own either.

8

LORENZO LED OSCAR, APRIL AND JULIAN THROUGH THE AIRPORT until they reached a passenger lounge outside security.

He went to open the door, paused, then turned to them.

"Please, be careful as to what you expect."

"What do you mean?" replied Oscar, keen to go in and meet the new Sensitives.

"They are unlike any of you. They know little of their gift or what they can do. I imagine they are quite scared."

"I'm not surprised if they know what's at stake. I'm sure we'll manage."

With a smile that was entirely forced, Lorenzo led them in, Oscar first, with April by his side and Julian trailing behind.

"This is Sebastian." Lorenzo indicated a young man, sat back in a chair with his right foot on his left knee and his arm draped over the empty seat next to him.

"Call me Seb," he said as he stood up. He slicked back his thick, black hair before offering his hand to Oscar. Seb held eye contact without saying anything, just continuing to shake Oscar's hand. He had a faraway look in his eye as if he knew something, as if he had some secret he was hiding. He was supremely good-looking, with distinctly Italian features and skin perfectly unblemished. "This better be good. I was just about to lay down with a Greek goddess when this guy showed up." He nodded his head toward Lorenzo.

"And who might this be?" asked Seb, noticing April. He took her hand and kissed it before giving her a gentle wink. Oscar was proud of himself for not being jealous – a few years ago, yes, but after all he and April had been through, there would be very little that could break them apart now.

"My name is April," she snapped, taking her hand away. "And I think you should be a little more respectful toward someone who is going to be your teacher."

"I do apologise," Seb responded, accompanied by a grin that indicated his apology was anything but genuine.

"And this is…?" Seb asked, offering his hand to Julian.

Julian kept his hands in his pockets and looked at Seb like he was dirt.

Oscar shook his head. He knew Julian was angry, but acting like this wasn't helping.

Eventually, Julian did respond, taking the hand and engaging in a brief handshake.

"Julian," he answered.

"Julian. Nice to meet you."

"And this," Lorenzo interrupted, pointing at a girl sat down, staring at her feet, "is Madison."

"Madison?" Oscar repeated, offering a hand out to her. She glanced at him timidly, limply shook his hand, then turned away. "And do you have a shortened name, or is Maddison okay?"

"Maddie, sir," she spoke, in a voice so quiet it could barely be heard.

April sat down next to her.

"My name's April," she said, her voice soft and reassuring. "And I've heard you're a gifted conduit. Is that right?"

43

Maddie fiddled with one of her hoodie strings with her teeth. She stared off into the distance. Oscar had a feeling this wasn't rudeness, but shyness – this girl had evidently been through a lot.

"That's what they tell me," Maddie finally answered with a small-town American accent.

"Well, so am I. I look forward to helping you."

Oscar turned to Lorenzo, putting his back to the conversation between Maddie and April.

"She okay?" Oscar asked.

"Her parents are deeply religious," Lorenzo answered. "A few months ago, she started speaking with the voice of her dead grandfather, then claimed she couldn't remember a thing about it. Her parents didn't react too well, and they sent her away to a church boarding school. It was only recently the school learnt the real reason she was sent away, and they got in touch with us."

Oscar looked out at the rest of the Sensitives. Seb, sat back and fiddling coolly with his sunglasses; April engaged in an encouraging conversation with Maddie; and Julian stood behind him, looking anywhere but at Oscar.

So here they were.

The Sensitives.

The beginning of the group that were supposedly going to eradicate a multitude of demons, the number of which the world had never seen before, in a record time that the world had also never seen before.

"*The 15:40 aeroplane to East Midlands Airport is now boarding at gate thirty.*"

"That's us," Oscar observed. "I guess we'd better go."

Oscar offered a hand out to Lorenzo.

"Thank you for your help," he said.

Reluctantly, Lorenzo took it. Despite being such a small

gesture, this meant a lot to Oscar – it was a sign that, after all the apologies and the rants, they had his support.

"We will search for more Sensitives. We will send them your way."

"Please do. And, if you could find some good ones, that would be great."

They both chuckled at the joke, then the chuckle died down and the graveness of the situation grew immediately apparent.

"Good luck," Lorenzo said.

With that, they picked up Seb and Maddie's luggage, and made their way to their gate.

9

AFTER INITIALLY BEING ANXIOUS ABOUT MEETING OSCAR, JULIAN, and April, Maddie had then been anxious about boarding the plane. Now she'd boarded the plane, she was anxious about who she'd have to sit by, and whether she would be able to find anything to talk to them about, or whether the normal uncomfortable silence people tend to share with her would persist.

As it was, Oscar, Julian, and April all sat in three seats together, leaving Maddie to sit with Seb. She wasn't sure about it him, especially having been trapped in a room with him for hours. He seemed to stare, with a weird glint in his eyes, like he was thinking something he shouldn't and he was enjoying it.

As they took off, she watched the three who would be mentoring her, watching them deep in conversation. Well, the two that called themselves Oscar and April, anyway – the other one, Julian, just seemed to sit there scowling. She wondered why he was so angry, whether he'd fallen out with the others or if that was just his normal, grumpy self.

Despite her apprehension, the strangeness of the situation felt less strange than it ever had. As if she wasn't crazy or broken – and these things were real.

She thought back to the night when she'd fallen off her chair, then opened her eyes to find her parents staring at her with wide, dumbfounded eyes. They'd sent her away so quickly, she'd barely been able to understand what she could do.

Then it kept happening.

Some teachers thought it may be mental illness. Some of the religiously devout thought it may be spiritual influence – but most thought she was just some stroppy teenage girl who didn't 'live on the same world as them,' as they would put it. She supposed they were right, in a way. She'd often stare out the window, not listening to a single word of class, then find herself intentionally put on the spot by a teacher who noticed her lack of attention.

Then, just when she least expected it or least wanted it, it happened.

She lost control. She felt absent from her body, even though she was still in it. Like something was in her, speaking for her, and she was watching it. Like her body was a car and she was in the backseat, and someone else was turning the wheel.

At first, it was small. Just a few times, and very briefly.

But, more and more recently, she was beginning to worry that she'd be condemned to the backseat forever.

And now she was being called a…what was it April said?

A *conduit*.

She liked April. Not just because she looked cool – had funky hair and jewellery and a kooky fashion sense, one that Maddie would never dare embrace, as it would prevent her from sinking into the background and remaining unnoticed – but because she seemed to care.

And because she said she was the same.

She was a conduit, too.

And maybe April could tell her how to control it.

"Stop staring at them, it's weird," blurted Seb, and she only just realised he was staring at her.

"Sorry," she responded in a voice that sounded like it was trapped in a box. She turned to look out the window.

Seb laughed a brief snort of laughter at her expense, then pushed some of his beautiful locks out of his flawless face. She watched his reflection, guiltily aware of how good-looking he was.

"So what do you reckon, then?" Seb asked. "Our new hosts. These... Sensitives."

Maddie knew she should respond, but didn't. The words failed her, as they often did. Noticing him looking at her expectantly, she simply shrugged, but with the smallest movement she could.

"You're not much of a talker, are you?" Seb observed.

"No," Maddie said, unsure whether it had been heard.

"I reckon they seem full of it. I mean, I believe all this shit an' all that; it's a good explanation as to why these things keep happening – but really? Exorcisms? How sweet! I mean, I can't wait to see it."

He left space in the conversation for Maddie to speak, but she didn't take it.

"And that April," he said, sneering as he stared at the back of her head.

"I think she's with Oscar," Maddie said, surprising herself at being so forceful – well, forceful for her, anyway.

"Yeah, I know. Still, I'm sure there'll be plenty of them in England. Not quite like what I had in Italy, but it'll do. I wonder how much the ladies go for an exorcist. Whether it's a turn-on."

"I wouldn't imagine so."

"Why not?"

"Well – because the only people who perform exorcisms aside from Sensitives, are priests."

He grinned at her.

"How do you know so much?" he asked.

She shrugged and turned back to the window.

"You know, I like it when you talk," he said. "You're always so quiet. I mean, I barely know you, but I see you're all shy and that. But when you talk, and you put me in my place – I like it. I do."

She didn't know what to say. She forced a smile at him, hoping that would be enough to shut him up, and kept her eyes on the clouds passing by.

"Still, this should be a bit of fun," he said, leaning his head back and closing his eyes. "Wake me up when we get there. Unless my dream's a good one, that is."

Grateful for the silence, she continued to think about April, and being a conduit, and what she might be able to do.

10

OSCAR SAT BACK IN HIS CHAIR AND HUFFED – A LONG, AUDIBLE, stress-releasing huff.

It had been a long, long day.

Julian had always been the one doing all that Oscar was doing. Talking to the Vatican, discussing with Lorenzo, showing Maddie and Seb to their rooms – but it seemed that Julian's grudge prevented him from taking on the responsibilities he normally would.

This meant that Oscar had to take the lead; and it felt as if Julian somehow expected him to.

Maybe that's why Julian was taking a step back; because it was Oscar's mess, and Julian saw it as his role to clean it up.

Or, maybe Julian really was that deeply angry at Oscar that he was unable to talk without spewing venomous retorts.

Or, maybe Julian was being Julian. As adept with his skills as he was, he had always been quite blunt and short-tempered, especially when it came to Oscar.

The new recruits hadn't filled Oscar with hope. He'd shown Maddie to her room with her barely looking at him. She seemed to keep her head down and shuffle into the room with her responses to his questions coming out in a soft mutter.

Seb, on the other hand, sauntered through the house with an arrogance that would suggest he owned it. He'd flashed his winning smile as he began unpacking, placing his clothes in the wardrobe and his posters on the wall, already making the room his own.

Then, as Oscar walked past Maddie's room once more, he glanced at her, and she was already buried in a book.

He paused, recalling when Hayley used to sleep in that room.

Well, the thing that disguised itself as Hayley did, anyway.

He wondered if staying in this room would cause any problems for Maddie; whether that would mean she'd unwillingly channel something she didn't want to. He guessed they'd find out.

Oscar made himself a cup of tea and sat at the kitchen table. He leant his head on his arm and somehow found his eyes closing.

"Oscar," April said, entering the room with Julian following behind, prompting Oscar to sit up. "Julian is ready to share his theory now."

Julian turned back to April and shook his head, directing himself back toward the door. April grabbed Julian's arm and whispered, "You promised."

"Come on," Oscar urged. "We need to hear it."

Julian sighed, poised between April and the door.

"Julian, if we want to do anything, you need to share it with both of us," April urged him, speaking like one would to a petulant child.

"I've shared it with *you*," Julian grumbled.

"Yes, and now you need to share it with Oscar."

"Julian," Oscar tried. "How long can this silent treatment go on for?"

Julian scoffed and shook his head, as if this was the most ridiculous question he'd ever been asked.

"He's been reading Derek's journals," April said, nudging Julian to speak up. "And he's been researching a bit about Sensitives, and what they are, and how they were created."

"We know how they were created," Oscar said. "Conceived by Heaven, wasn't it?"

Julian moved his head from side to side, suggesting that Oscar was on the right track, but not quite.

"Then what?" Oscar prompted.

Julian remained stuck in his position, poised between speaking and going.

"I need to know, Julian."

"Fine," Julian grunted, but didn't look at Oscar once during his explanation. "It is correct to say that Sensitives were conceived by Heaven, and that piece of Heaven that remains in them is what gives them their gift. But it seems as if the levels may be outweighed in some Sensitives compared to others."

"What do you mean?"

Julian sighed, again hesitant to engage, but continued with his eyes rooted to the floor.

"Some end up having very little power. They may, for example, see something out the corner of their eye, or just feel something brush past their leg, but never know what it is. They are Sensitives with very little of their gift, and will most likely live their lives without ever knowing. Actual Sensitives...we have more than that, which is why we can do what we can do."

"But what does–"

Julian raised his hand to indicate not to interrupt.

"Theoretically," he continued, "this means that there must be something that evens the scale. So, if those with very small of their gift have little, and we have, say, a medium amount – there must be someone who has more. Who has too much."

"Too much?"

"Yes. Someone who is extremely powerful. And, if left unhinged and untrained, potentially dangerous. They would be very susceptible to the demonic attacks; but, then again, would also be able to manipulate demons with far more ease than you or I can."

"So you think there is this person out there?"

"I'm certain of it."

Oscar sat on the edge of his chair, possibilities rushing through his thoughts, trying to quell his excitement.

"So," Oscar summarised, "If we were to find that person – they could be a big factor in what we're doing. They could exorcise demons at a higher rate. And with the amount of possessions becoming what it is, well…I mean…They could potentially decide this."

"That's the theory."

"Then how–"

"No!" Julian barked. "I've told you my theory. Now I'm going to bed."

He punched the door against the wall and stormed out. Talking to Oscar for so long had evidently been far more than he was prepared to tolerate.

Ignoring the outburst, which Oscar was becoming averse to, he stood and walked over to April. He took her in his arms and gave her a gentle kiss.

"If this is true…" Oscar mused.

"Yes," April confirmed. "It could change everything."

"But this person… Where do we even start?"

11

HISTORY CLASS WAS AS MUNDANE AS IT ALWAYS WAS – EXCEPT, Thea didn't really notice. Her eyes were directed out of the window, in hope that she wouldn't see anything strange around her classmates or her teacher.

She'd always seen these things. Around many corners, she'd often stumble upon a grim face, or a difficult mess, or a dark omen. These corners, however, would normally occur every few months or so.

In the past few weeks, they seemed to be occurring every few hours.

And she was struggling to cope.

It wasn't just the mental torment, the strain on her mind, the way the sights made her head feel like her brain was growing and bursting against her skull. Nor was it just the sight of violence, the constant, contorted chaos that decorated these people, or the sights of creatures that appeared to be not of this world – creatures full of claws and red eyes and shapes so desperately unnatural. Nor was it even the constant frequency with which they were now choosing to bother her.

It was the way that each of them made her wonder what

was happening to Ben. Whether these things were of some other world, and whether these things were tormenting Ben in this world.

Hell, maybe they weren't even of another world. If she spoke aloud what she'd seen, she knew she'd receive immediate psychiatric help. Maybe that was what she needed.

Or maybe, it wasn't.

She huffed, burying her head in her arms, so fed up with mulling over the same thoughts, the same conundrums, the same conflicts; creating the same anxious unease that bashed around her mind like a battered boxer against a ring.

She wished it would all just...stop.

Be quiet.

That everything, even if just for a minute, would stop attacking her. Her thoughts would stop shouting, her eyes would stop witnessing, her body would stop racing tired adrenaline around her weary body.

"Thea?"

She looked up, darting her eyes around, wondering what creature was calling her name this time.

To her surprise, it was her teacher.

"Thea, is everything okay?" her teacher asked.

She looked around. All of her sixth-form colleagues were staring at her. Those same judgemental stares, those same stares that people tried to make look neutral but Thea knew weren't. She could practically hear their thoughts from their mocking faces.

What's wrong with her?

Why is she so weird?

This is all just because of her mental brother...

"He's not mental!" Thea burst out.

Confused faces peered back at her.

Who was she talking to? To herself?

Suddenly, she was so tired. Those nights without sleep

caught up with her. Those nights lying awake, staring at the ceiling, wishing she could stop seeing shadows move and faces stare.

"I..." Thea went to speak, but her voice got lost somewhere on its way to her lips.

"Are you sure you should be here?" the teacher asked, putting on a concerned face, such a good Samaritan, such a fucking saviour. "You know, considering..."

Who was this teacher to talk about him?

Of course, her teachers wouldn't talk about him directly – no one would. It was referred to as *the incident*, or *what happened*, or *the tragedy...*

"My brother died," Thea bluntly stated, fed up with people dancing around the subject. "Is that what you are referring to?"

A wave of dreaded discomfort passed along every face. Now they weren't staring at her. They were looking away, hoping not to engage, hoping they wouldn't have to talk about it. They didn't know what to say, what to do, and Thea got that; but she was sick of it. No one ever knew what to say or do, herself included. So why was everyone pretending?

"I really think–" her teacher went to speak.

"I don't care what you think," Thea said, dropping her head back into her arms. What she'd give to fall asleep.

"Thea, can you lift your head up, please?"

Thea did not.

Thea...

That's when they started.

Ben has a message...

"*Shut up!*" she screamed, lifting her head.

They were everywhere. The room was full of them. Beside every table, behind every student, in every spare space. Same grim faces, same dead eyes, same demented, sinister stares.

And they were all staring at her.

"Leave me alone..." she whimpered, wishing she wasn't

crying, wishing these things would go.

The teacher said something but she didn't hear it. It was muffled by the bodies surrounding the room that only she saw.

"Please…"

In complete unison, each of them lifted their arms. Slowly and limply, their fingers stretched and pointed at her.

"No…"

Their cracked lips curved into smiles that displayed their bloody fangs.

"No!" she screamed, closing her eyes and covering her face, turning toward the wall.

"Thea!" her teacher's voice shouted.

She turned. Opened her eyes. They were gone, and her teacher was stood over her.

"Thea, snap out of it!" the teacher persisted, putting on a caring voice that reeked of impatience.

"Snap out of it?" Thea repeated.

Sure.

Yeah.

That's all she had to do.

Snap the hell out of it.

"Thea–"

"Leave me alone!" she shouted, standing and pushing her teacher out the way. She scooped her books and pencil case haphazardly into her bag, placed it over her shoulder and marched out of the classroom.

They were all waiting for her in the corridor.

Lining the walls like an ovation waiting to applaud her exit.

But there was no applause. Just hands raised and pointed, directed at her; their stares, their deadened stares, all of them focussed on her…

She bowed her head, covered her ears, and kept her eyes on the floor as she rushed down the corridor and out of the school.

12

MENTAL ASYLUMS DO NOT EXIST ANYMORE, OR SO OSCAR thought.

Such a way of referring to a building is dated, mostly reduced to comics with extreme super-villains or books that sit on an ageing shelf with decades-old dust.

Nowadays, we have psychiatric units, rather than broken-down buildings for the criminally insane with a cliched lightning bolt striking the sky behind it.

Yet, as Oscar looked up at St. Helen's Psychiatric Unit, he felt he had gone back in time. The sad fact was that, in the past month, many people had performed violent acts without any rationality behind them; people with no history of violence and no reason for what they had done. As a result, so many people had been deemed as mentally unhinged that they'd had to dedicate a psychiatric unit entirely to them.

Oscar, however, knew the truth – they were not mentally unhinged.

He looked to Maddie and Seb stood between him and April and Julian.

Maddie looked scared – but she seemed to be scared of

everything. Seb had his permanent air of confidence, but Oscar could see his hands fidgeting.

"Do we understand what is expected of all of us?" Oscar asked, directed at Maddie and Seb.

"Yes," Maddie said, nodding.

Oscar looked to Seb.

"Yeah, I get it," Seb replied. "Don't say a thing, just watch. I just – I didn't think this kind of thing really existed, you know?"

Oscar couldn't help but smile. It took him back to his first experiences of exorcism, and how quickly his scepticism had been overturned.

"Trust me," Oscar said. "After today, you'll never doubt it again."

As they entered, the temperature seemed to plummet. Despite still being daytime outside, the windows let in little light. A dark blue-hue seemed to tint every wall, making the cold feel even colder.

"I'm here to see Margaret Kummings," Oscar told the receptionist. "There's supposed to be a room prepared for us."

The receptionist nodded.

"I would take you there," she told him, "but you can go on your own. It's up the stairs, down the corridor, and third door on the right."

Oscar smiled in confirmation. He understood the receptionist not wanting to accompany them and, in a way, was glad of it – it meant that Maddie and Seb got to see the true fear demonic possession prompted.

"As you probably heard," Oscar said as they made their way upstairs, "the subject's name is Margaret Kummings. She is seventy-three years old, a retired nurse. She was awarded with commendations for her services to medicine last year, six years after her retirement. She has a husband who says she's never said an unpleasant word to anybody, and two children who say she's a fantastic, caring grandmother."

"Then why are we here?" asked Seb as they paused by the door.

"Because last week she stabbed her grandson in his stomach with a turkey baster and defecated on his corpse. Shall we?"

Oscar opened the room, his breath visible in the air. The poor light overhead lit the sterile, neutral walls. Their footsteps echoed around the room like a bathroom, and it was immediately obvious that everything but the bed had been removed from the room.

The subject herself, Margaret Kummings, lay on the bed, squirming. Her wrists were restrained to the headboard, her hospital gown stuck to her body with dried sweat and stuck to her crotch with dried blood.

Oscar placed his bag down, opened it, and withdrew his rosary. After placing it around his neck, he took out his cross and the Rites of Exorcism.

"Stay there," he told Seb and Maddie, pointing at the corner of the room. April went with them and stood beside them, offering a reassuring smile. She put her arm around Maddie, whispering that it was going to be okay.

Oscar looked to Julian, who stood beside Oscar but a little further back. Even under the circumstances, Julian did not return his gaze.

Oscar didn't have time to care. He made his way to the end of the bed and looked at the lecherous grin adorning the pale face and cracked lips of what was once a gentle, kind nurse.

"Hello, Margaret," he said. "I know this isn't Margaret in front of me, but I know that you are in there. I just want you to know that we're here to help."

Margaret laughed. They always do. Always a low-pitched, growling laugh. Oscar was honestly sick of it. They were all the same – he was yet to meet a demon that surprised him or broke from the norm.

"Now, I address the demon who dwells within."

The demon inside immediately responded with a deep, croaking exhale of breath. Her body rose into the air, just her restrained wrists remaining on the bed.

Seb and Maddie gasped. Oscar didn't look at them, but subconsciously acknowledged it – there's nothing like a levitating woman to show you that it was all real.

"Demon, I would like your name."

The demon continued floating its legs into the air until Margaret's body was completely upside down, flattened against the wall.

Its head turned, rotating fully without its body moving, until it was looking Oscar in the eyes in an unnaturally impossible position.

Now this was new.

Oscar had never seen *that* before.

"In the name of God, I demand you, demon, tell me your name."

Oscar was taken off his feet. Before he could realise what was happening, he'd been flung across the room, punched into the far wall, and dropped to the floor.

He lifted his hand to his head, feeling the cut, blood trickling from his forehead to his lips.

This was also new.

Oscar tried to stand but found himself pushed back into the wall once more, his head slamming. He dropped to the ground, groggy, concussed.

"Oscar!" April gasped, but Oscar raised his arm, indicating for her to stay where she was.

He stayed on his knees, willing the blurs to leave his eyesight, willing coherent thoughts to return.

He had to save face in front of Maddie and Seb. He couldn't let them think this was anything unusual.

But this was unusual.

A demon who had been amalgamized could do this, yes – but this woman had shown no signs of possession before a few weeks ago...

Oscar knew what this meant.

That there was strength in numbers.

That the quantity improved the quality.

That they were facing a legion of demons like no other.

13

FIVE YEARS.

It had been five years since Elijah had become a psychiatric nurse.

He had experienced all kinds of people. All kinds of illnesses, all kinds of challenges. He'd had to restrain more people than he'd liked, had to clean up more faeces than he'd expected, and suffer more setbacks from patients he cared about than he'd ever admit.

Somehow, more had occurred in the past few weeks than had occurred in the past five years.

And now, walking through the corridors, rubbing his goose-pimpled arms, he listened to the nonsensical ramblings coming from every room he passed. All spewing nonsense he didn't understand.

"Mors venit! Mors venit! Mors venit!" from his right.

"Ante arcum diabolil! Ante acrum diabolic!" from his left.

He walked into the bathroom, the only place where the noise was a distant buzz, and stopped by the sink. He washed his hands, repeatedly, hoping to remove the grease of a twelve-hour shift.

He was meant to go home four hours ago, but he had still been needed, and his dedication to his job meant he could never leave his colleagues to deal with helpless patients alone.

The sight of his reflection met him with disgust. Bags punched the skin beneath his eyelids, bloodshot eyes startled him, and an unkempt, greasy mop atop his head accompanied the stench of the hospital.

He wondered if he even smelt it that much anymore, and whether those beside him at the bus stop or coffee shop could smell it more. That smell of sweaty piss, aged cafeteria food and disgruntled, clammy patients.

He filled his hands with water and splashed it over his face, drenching his skin with mildly warm water. He'd hoped it would wake him up a bit, but it didn't. It clung to his face with an uncomfortable damp.

A scream sounded outside the room.

He didn't react. It wasn't anything abnormal.

He wondered how much he'd had to experience in order to become a person that didn't react to a nearby scream.

But it wasn't just one. It was more.

It was a barricade of noise, a bombardment of piercing distress.

He made his way out of the bathroom and into the corridor, where he paused, listening, curious.

All around him, from every room, every patient was screaming, battering against their bed, banging against the walls.

Through the doors nurses ran, doctors, security, even – flooding into various rooms, then rushing out and into another room. It seemed like every patient was going crazy, celebrating something with a sense of irony, a sense of undeterred violence.

He walked slowly through, looking through the narrow glass of the first wall. An elderly man, barely able to walk two steps alone, was kicking out at the orderlies with such venom they were sent to their backs.

Walking along to the next pane of glass, a four-year-old child snapped its jaws at the doctor through its high-pitched scream.

The same happened in the next.

And the next.

And the next.

And the next.

Something was happening in the hospital to wake the crazies, and Elijah couldn't think what it could be.

14

OSCAR COULD FEEL MADDIE AND SEB'S EYES BURNING THE BACK of his head. He could feel the truth cascading over them like an ice-cold bucket of water, and he could almost smell their fear.

But he could smell his own more.

He could feel it pushing against him, fighting against his body, like the wind at the top of a hill in the middle of a riotous storm; and with all that he resisted, the force pushed back on him with just as much vigour.

The swollen vessel that was once Margaret's face leered back at him.

"Struggling?" its scabbed lips mouthed.

Oscar curled his nose in defiance, looked to his side where Julian was, and waited for support.

Julian simply stood with his arm across his face, shielding himself, not even bothering to look.

Oscar had no choice but to begin the rites. Without the demon's name he was going to struggle, but he was fighting against too much power – he had to do something to weaken it.

"Holy Mother of God, Holy Virgin of virgins, all holy angels and archangels – hear me," Oscar said.

He awaited the call.

It was not forthcoming.

"Julian!" Oscar shouted.

Julian ignored him.

"Julian, dammit – the call!"

Julian met his stare, but found himself taken off his feet once he did, pulled backwards by his dangling leg and thrown against the far door.

"Julian, this is useless without a response!"

"Have mercy on us!" April shouted, filling in where Julian should.

Imbecile, Oscar thought.

"God the Holy Spirit, Holy Trinity, graciously hear us."

"Have mercy on us!" April said, encouraging Maddie and Seb to join in.

"All holy saints of God intercede for us, from all lewdness, from lightning and tempest."

"Have mercy on us!" shouted April, with Maddie's unexpected voice projected with hers and Seb's desperate voice trailing behind.

Good. This was good. Even if Julian was being unresponsive – Maddie and Seb's strengthening beliefs would help strengthen their fight.

"Lord, have mercy on us!"

"Have mercy on us!"

It still wasn't enough.

Oscar looked to Julian and shouted above the violent wind still attacking him.

"Julian, I need you, too! Have mercy on us!"

Julian looked back at Oscar with deadened eyes.

"Julian, the response!"

Nothing.

"Julian, I need it now!"

Reluctantly, his lips moved. "Have mercy on–"

His response was cut short.

He was taken from his feet, lifted through the air by his foot, and left to dangle like a helpless rat by its tail. He fought against it, screamed, struggled, but the demon only cackled in response.

Oscar looked to the demon's eyes.

Looked to its restraints unhooking themselves from its wrists.

This was *not* good.

"Deliver our souls from–"

From his feet he was sent across the room. Only, he wasn't being pushed, he was being pulled – and he found himself travelling faster than he could acknowledge toward the rotting face of the liberated demon inhabiting Margaret.

Its hands were free – bruised and cracked, but they were free.

It tucked its stubby fingers around Oscar's throat and looked him dead in the eyes.

"Oscar Martinez…" it mockingly acknowledged.

"Grant us eternal rest, O Lord," Oscar tried, but its other hand simply covered his mouth.

"How I'd like to be inside you…"

"Julian!" April screamed. Oscar was unable to see her, but she heard it in her voice – that true fear that he'd only ever heard a few times. He'd heard it when their demonic daughter had manipulated him to attempted murder, and now he heard it once again.

"We need to retreat!" Julian finally decided, all too late. "This is too much!"

Its face grew closer to his, and its mouth stretched, as if it was about to wrap itself around the whole of Oscar's head. Its putrid breath choked him as much as its tightening grip on his gullet and he looked into its eyes, seeing that he was helpless to stop what it wished to do.

It screamed, lifting its head back and wailing, and dropped Oscar. Behind it, Julian stood with his cross against its back.

"Get the kids out of here!" Oscar demanded, prioritising them above all else. They scurried past him, and Julian followed them.

April grabbed hold of Oscar's hand and pulled him away. Margaret screeched as it reached out for his leg, but April pulled him from its grasp. He hit the floor and, just as he felt himself about to be pulled back to the demon, he scrambled into the corridor. He locked the door and bolted it as many times as the number of bolts would allow.

Oscar slumped against the far wall, choking on his own breath, doing all he could to try and calm his panting.

The demon...

It had taken him off the floor...

It had brought him toward it...

How the hell had it done that?

April helped Oscar to his feet.

He slowly realised that everyone was staring at him.

Maddie.

Seb.

April.

Julian.

With a scowl, Oscar went to speak, ready to direct his most pertinent and angriest of thoughts at Julian, but April squeezed his hand.

"Now's not the time," she urged him.

He nodded. She was right – but this was not over. He lifted his finger and jabbed it in Julian's direction.

"But there will be a time," Oscar said, knowing he would not be in control of his fury if he did not have April there to keep him grounded. "There will. And we will be having an exchange of words."

Julian looked back at Oscar, unperturbed, as if considering what to say. In the end, he turned to the others, and simply said, "It's time we left."

April tightened her grip on Oscar's hand.

Oscar was not a confrontational person. He had always lacked aggression and a backbone, and the new-found self-confidence April had helped him find still didn't change that. But, bit by bit, all good will and patience was starting to creep to the back of his mind.

"Come on," she urged him. "I'm mad too, but we need to go."

With her by his side, he joined the rest in fleeing the building.

THEN

15

JULIAN SAID IT AGAIN WITH MORE CONVICTION – BUT STILL never enough conviction for Derek.

"From all evil deliver us, O Lord."

"Louder!" barked Derek.

"From all evil deliver us, O Lord!" Julian repeated, with more volume but just as little vigour.

"With more oomph!"

"From all evil deliver us, O Lord!" Julian repeated again, shouting louder.

"No, no, no, no, no!" Derek said, standing and waving his arms. He faced the far fence of the garden, resting his open fingers on his forehead.

Julian threw his arms into the air, remonstrating his frustration that still didn't match Derek's.

"I don't get it!" Julian exclaimed. "These are just words."

Derek swung around and jabbed his finger at Julian.

"That is where you are wrong!" he retorted with anger Julian rarely saw. "These are not just words. And if you say them just as words, then you will not find a favourable response."

"From who? God?"

"If that is indeed who we are praying to, then, for the sake of argument, yes. Fine. God."

"But…"

Julian didn't say it.

He chose the better option – to be quiet.

Unfortunately, Derek knew exactly what Julian was going to say.

"You still don't believe, do you?"

"It's not like that."

"Yes, it is. It is *precisely* like that. You don't believe in any of this."

"I guess not."

"Then what the heck are you doing here? Why waste my time?"

Julian sighed. Put his hands on his hips. Considered that question.

"I don't know."

"If you really didn't believe it then, trust me, you would have left," Derek insisted. "It's not belief that's faltering. It's your energy. You quite clearly do not care."

"It's not that, Derek. It's just – these words mean nothing to me. They are just prayers; what's their point?"

Derek sat on his garden bench, slumped as much as Derek would ever slump with his unfaltering posture.

"Sit," Derek instructed.

Julian trudged over and sat by Derek. Derek lifted the Rites of Exorcism and placed it on Julian's lap, ignoring Julian's eye roll in protestation.

"Read the line again," Derek instructed.

Julian hesitated. Wondered whether to bother. Then decided it was best to appease him.

"From all evil deliver us, O Lord."

"What does evil mean?"

"What?"

What kind of stupid question was that?

"What does *evil* mean?" Derek repeated, with more insistence.

"It… It means…"

Julian was surprised to find it a quite difficult concept to explain.

"It means bad," Julian said. "The worst things in the world. The things that power every nasty act."

"Exactly! And what powers every nasty act? What is the epitome of evil? What guides all the horrific acts of human nature?"

"…Hell?"

"Yes!" Derek practically jumped for joy. He was never as passionate or animated about anything as he was when explaining the demonic to Julian. "Hell creates evil, and Hell creates the demon you are fighting. What does deliver mean?"

"Er…"

"Hurry up, what does it mean?"

"Deliver means to move something to somewhere else, to let something go."

"Precisely – you are asking your powers of good to let you go from the creation of evil, and to let the victim of the demon go from the creation of evil. Is that not a request that deserves some passion?"

"I guess…"

"You guess? Julian, you are requesting the saving of a person's soul. You know what these words mean now, yes?"

"Yeah…"

"Then get up and say them."

Julian stood. He went to speak.

"No, there's not enough room here!" interjected Derek. "In the middle of the garden!"

With a huff, Julian stepped away from the bench and stood in the middle of the garden.

He went to speak but was interrupted again.

"Before you deliver it this time, I would like you to take a moment to think about it. To think about what you are asking."

Julian nodded.

"Close your eyes."

Julian did so.

"Someday you are going to lead a group of Sensitives into battle. You are not only going to be praying for your soul, but for theirs. You are going to need to know what every one of these words means."

Julian didn't nod. He didn't need to.

"Now," Derek said. "Again."

Julian opened his eyes.

Looked sincerely toward his mentor.

And he delivered the line with the most passion Derek had ever heard it delivered.

NOW

16

AFTER SEEING MADDIE AND SEB TO THEIR ROOMS, APRIL MADE her way back downstairs to the kitchen, where she found Julian and Oscar in tense silence. Julian leant against the kitchen side, waiting for a boiling kettle, whilst Oscar sat on the edge of a chair, his leg shaking – both of them looking away from each other.

April closed the door behind her.

"Right, guys," she said. "We really need to sort this out."

No one said anything.

"Honestly," she tried. "I think we need to–"

"What the *hell* was that!" Oscar said, standing and accidentally knocking his chair over. April was shocked – she'd never seen this in him before. Oscar looked as if he'd even surprised himself. He stood with his hands on his hips, shaking his head, facing away.

April turned to Julian.

"Well?" she asked.

"You're kidding, right?" Julian asked.

Oscar turned and looked at him, reddening.

"Kidding?" Oscar growled.

"Oscar, calm down," April urged him.

"Kidding? What the *fuck* would we be kidding about?"

"Do you want to watch how you talk to me?" Julian snapped.

"You could have gotten me killed! I know you don't seem to care about whether such a thing happens, you never have – but there were three other people in there as well. Including April, who, I understood, you supposedly care for quite a bit!"

"Don't you dare–"

"Don't I dare what?"

"I took April off the goddamn streets! I gave her a bloody home! A life!"

"Yeah, well today you almost saw that life taken away."

"Oscar," April said, putting a hand on his back, but it went unnoticed.

"All you had to do was a response. As we've always done. *Always*. And you didn't. And because of that, because of your own personal feelings, you put *everything* in jeopardy – including the only chance we have to–"

Julian's laughter interrupted Oscar's ranting.

"What?" Oscar demanded.

"It's just, the irony."

"What are you talking about?"

"You telling me about how personal feelings are screwing everything up."

"It's time we–"

"What!" This time it was Julian's turn to shout. "Time we what? Actually confronted the issue, actually talk about what you did, about how much you messed everything up?"

Oscar and April responded with stony silence.

"This is all because of *you*. The fate of the world is fucked – because of *you*! Never forget that. *Ever*."

"I don't forget it–"

"But you have! You think my grievance with you is some

little grudge – no, it is not. It is not a falling out that will be repaired with an apology. It is a grudge that will never go away, because it is something that will never be forgiven!"

Oscar went to speak, but no legitimate response found its way out.

"So yeah, I am pissed off. Rightly so. The whole world should be! And you, running around, pretending to be Mr Good Guy, pretending to act like you're in charge, being all noble, fixing everything – it convinces everyone else, but not me!" His arms gestured wildly. "Because I know what you are. What you did. I was there, and you know what the worst thing is, the real worst thing – I saw it coming."

"Julian–"

"Now there's no more future for us. For anyone. No more birthdays. You two won't get to celebrate your bloody amazing anniversary whilst I stand by knowing what a crock of shit it is – because there will be no more anniversaries. Nothing. There will be nothing. Because of *you*, Oscar. And *you* alone."

Oscar bowed his head.

The kettle finished boiling.

"So you ask me why I don't talk to you," Julian said, ceasing his shouting and replacing it with disappointment. "You ask me why I can't find a way to move past this. Because there is no moving past this, Oscar. Any bit of respect I had for you, any I'd grown or found – it left. And it is never coming back. Not after what you did."

Silence governed the room for the next ten minutes. Oscar found his way to a seat, where he gazed at nothing, his hand over his mouth, his leg anxiously bouncing.

Julian turned back to the kettle and poured himself a coffee, not offering one to anyone else.

April took a deep breath and decided to be the first one to end the silence.

"I care for you, Julian, I really do," she said. "We all know what caused this mess – but it is our duty to fix it. You get mad at Oscar for putting his feelings above the cause, but now you are doing the same, and if you can't stop, then…"

She trailed off. She couldn't say it.

"What?" Julian prompted. "Then what, April?"

"Then…maybe this isn't the best place for you to be. Maybe you should think about leaving."

Julian's face morphed from one emotion to the other. Blank absence staring coldly back at April, followed by ironic grins and head-shaking – finally ending in an affirmative, angry nod.

Only April would be able to see how much this hurt him.

He had done everything for her. He had taken her from the streets after she ran away from home. He taught her to harness her gift. He gave her food. He gave her a purpose.

But now, he was right. Mistakes would be created when they put their feelings above the cause.

And it hurt her deeply to have to say it.

Julian took his coffee and walked to the door, stopping as he passed April to look into the eyes of the girl he once knew.

"Go to Hell," he told her, and left the room.

April collapsed into the nearest seat. Oscar's arms were around her in an instant, pulling her close to his chest, feeling his t-shirt dampen from her tears.

He said nothing.

He just stroked her hair and held her, always knowing exactly what she needed.

Maddie and Seb sat on the top step, listening to every word.

"Wow," Seb finally said as the shouting began to lessen. "If they can't manage each other, what does that mean for us?"

Maddie shrugged. "I don't know."

"They seem like they are falling apart. How are we meant to learn from them when they are falling apart?"

A door slammed, and heavy footsteps approached the stairs. Julian appeared with a mug of coffee, and both of them tensed, worried he was going to scold them for eavesdropping. As it was, he didn't say a word. They both parted for him and he trudged past, across the corridor and into his room.

Maddie exchanged a glance with Seb.

"I don't know..." she said. "I just – he seems so angry. How are they supposed to help us?"

"What does he even do anyway?"

"I don't know."

"April seems all right. So does Oscar. Maybe we should just trust them."

"I want to. It's just... Did you see that thing?"

Seb didn't need to ask what she meant by *thing*.

"Yeah... I can't stop seeing it..."

Maddie knew what he meant. She hadn't been able to get that Margaret woman out of her mind since they left. She looked decrepit, as unhuman-like as a human could be – almost like a dying animal with predatory energy.

But what haunted her thoughts most was how they dealt with her.

Because yes, she was scary – but surely, the Sensitives being who they were, they would be able to defeat it. I mean, how many exorcisms had they supposedly done? Wasn't this what they did? Wasn't it their area of expertise?

It's like a plumber coming to fix your pipes and being chased away by those pipes – if that plumber was a demon-fighter and those pipes were a scary lady who could throw people off the ground and levitate.

And – what the hell was that about?

That woman had risen from the ground, right into the air. She had undone her own restraints. She had thrown Oscar and Julian around like they were rag dolls.

And this was *one* of them.

They were told there were going to be thousands, and they were going to have to fight thousands, and defeat them within a year – before something called *amalgamation incarnation* occurred.

She shook her head, ran her hands through her hair.

It was impossible.

She looked to Seb and could tell he'd been thinking exactly what she had.

"Maybe we should go," Maddie suggested.

"And do what? Go where?"

"I don't know, just...away."

"By the sound of it, there isn't any running from it. We could leave, but there's more of them."

"How do you know?"

She knew it was a silly question, as she'd have the same answer as Seb was about to give her.

"Because I feel it…"

A door opened downstairs. Oscar and April walked out into the corridor. Maddie and Seb both stood, about to rush back into their rooms, then realised they'd been noticed.

"I thought you two were in bed," April said, her voice soft. Her cheeks were puffy, like she'd been crying.

"We were just… chatting," Seb said, unable to think of a good excuse.

"It's two in the morning."

"Two in the morning is my prime time," he said, and Maddie wanted to giggle. At first, she'd found his cockiness annoying, but now she was starting to find it endearing.

"I'd get some rest," Oscar suggested. "We have another tough day tomorrow."

With a glance at each other and the raising of their eyebrows, Maddie and Seb silently acknowledged that rest was what they needed – even if they doubted they were going to get it.

So they bid each other good night and went to their separate beds for their own sleepless night.

18

EVERYONE WAS ALWAYS SO CONCERNED! EVERYONE CARED SO much it was almost sickening.

But, worst of all, everyone assumed it was because of her brother's death.

Thea was still devastated, yes – she still laid awake at night imagining scenarios where her brother just walked through the front door, alive. She still saw his face in children she walked past and spent hours in class wondering why oh why he did what he did.

But these problems had occurred far before her brother's death.

It was only now that it was getting worse, and it was only now that people were caring enough to notice.

"Thank you all for coming in," said Mrs Andrews, the head of sixth form. "I appreciate it's a hard time, and we are all concerned about Thea, which is why we're here."

Thea felt surrounded. Her mother sat to her left, her father to her right, and Mrs Andrews sat across the desk. As if this was some kind of interrogation or intervention where she was meant to open up and start talking about how hard life was and all that crap.

She had no intention of opening up whatsoever.

What, she was just supposed to tell them the things that she'd been seeing?

And what then?

How would they react? Where would they send her?

No. Some things were better left to the sanctity of the subconscious, where you can bury something for years at a time.

"I know things have been really hard for you, Thea," Mrs Andrews said without any idea as to how hard things had been for Thea. "And I'm surprised you've come back to school so soon. Would you consider a little more time off?"

Thea slumped in her seat and shrugged.

What benefit would more time off have?

How would her not coming to school so she could sit at home and ruminate all day possibly help her? How could sitting idly in her bedroom help, with little to occupy her mind and distract her thoughts from the spiralling madness she felt herself constantly falling further into?

As awful as this prisonous building was, it was all she had to keep her mind relatively busy.

"What about you, Mr and Mrs Kinsey? What are your thoughts?"

"Well," piped up her mother, "We are very concerned for Thea. And I'm sure these outbursts are linked to...recent events."

Recent events.

So that's what they were calling it.

Why?

Why not just say *her brother's violent suicide* and actually say what was happening?

This was why it was so ridiculous – she had to listen to the advice of people who couldn't even bring themselves to say what was going on.

"This is a very hard time for the family," her dad decided to volunteer, stating the very, very obvious in a way that made it seem as if he was stating something profound. "And maybe it would be an idea for Thea to see a psychiatrist, or a grief counsellor."

"How would you feel about that, Thea?" Mrs Andrews asked.

Thea ignored the question. She was too busy staring at a man over Mrs Andrews' shoulder.

"Thea?" she prompted, and looked over her shoulder to see what Thea was staring at, but found nothing.

Thea kept watching. The man was sad, whimpering almost. He was about Mrs Andrews' age, maybe a little younger. Half of his face was scarred in burns, and his right arm was twisted backwards.

"Thea, it would be good if you could say something," Mrs Andrews prompted.

Thea noticed that Mrs Andrews was wearing a wedding ring.

"Why do you still wear that ring?" Thea asked, quiet and monotone, knowing she shouldn't but unable to help herself.

"Sorry?" Mrs Andrews said.

"Your husband. How did he die?"

"Thea!" her mother exclaimed, but Thea ignored her.

"I know he had burns to the side of his face, and that he broke his arm backwards."

Mrs Andrews' jaw hung open, stuttering over her words.

"It was a car crash, wasn't it?" Thea asked.

"Thea, I really think–"

"He misses you a lot, you know. He cries often."

Mrs Andrews' face entwined between rage and understanding.

"Thea, what are you doing?" her mother asked again.

Thea looked around at all the confused, angry faces around her.

Then she looked to the lost face of the man stood behind Mrs Andrews, who looked toward her with grateful eyes, pleased that she was able to relay his message.

"Thea, this is really inappropriate," Mrs Andrews said. "We are trying to help you."

"This is exactly why you can't help me," Thea said, standing. "No one can."

She left the room and left the school, deciding to veto a lift from her parents and walk.

19

FACES STARED AT THEA BUT SHE NEVER STARED BACK.

Faces were the entry point to a person's soul.

Or, as she was worried – their lack of soul.

She saw too much in people's faces. She saw what was hidden beneath; she saw what was hiding behind them and she saw that, often, they weren't even really there.

Yet they were.

But only to her.

Pale faces. Eyes that either pled for comfort or fired anger. Expressions that were wounded with despair or wound up with aggression.

The dead always had such strong emotions. Well – those that she saw, anyway.

Assuming it was the dead.

Who else would it be?

What about those she saw in people who were living? Flickers of faces with scales and fangs – those weren't dead people, those weren't features people had. Those were things buried within people, most of whom either seemed unaware or incapable of concealing it.

She wrapped her arms around herself, pulling her hoodie close, tightening her grip for warmth. It was a small town, but it seemed full of people. Or, full of the dead – she didn't look up, so that way, she didn't know.

But still, she heard them.

Oh, how she wished she didn't hear them.

Help me...

Can you see me...

Please, you're the only one who seems to be listening...

"Leave me alone," she muttered. She was aware of faces turning in her direction as she spoke to what appeared to be nobody, and she willed herself to be quiet.

But you can help me...

Please...

Why won't you help me...

"I don't want to help you, just leave me alone!" She spoke without any realisation that words were passing her lips. Once it dawned on her that she was shouting, people began to stop, to look at her, to stare at this strange girl walking alone, huddled up, holding herself, getting wet in the rain, talking, shouting, saying things aloud to what appeared to be no one.

She didn't care.

After all of this, she just didn't care.

She wanted it to stop.

These things – why wouldn't they go?

We don't want to go...

Please just look at us...

We know you can hear us...

"Stop it!" she screamed, coming to a halt, dropping to her knees. She felt the bumps of the pavement cracks rip her jeans and she was bleeding but she didn't care.

She covered her ears.

But the smell... Like rotting meat... Like putrid flesh floating toward her in the rain...

Some good Samaritan put her hand on Thea's shoulder and asked if she was okay but Thea shrugged her off and screamed so hard her voice broke and her throat stung.

"Go away! Just go away!"

The person backed off and she could hear them speaking on the phone, to the police maybe, an ambulance, and she had to leave. The last thing she wanted was for someone who could lock her up to witness her having a mental breakdown in the middle of a rain-soaked street.

She stood and ran, kept her hands in her pockets, kept her hoodie wrapped around her although it did nothing she was soaking so wet so drenched her knee hurt it made her limp blood trickled down her shin and her shoes were falling apart she could feel the ground through the sole and she wanted people to stop staring at her why won't they stop staring please stop staring stop staring stop staring stop staring stop staring *stop!*

A face.

A woman.

She fell to her knees, seeing her before her. This wasn't like the dead; this was her mind's projection, and it was real. So real.

"Are you okay?" the woman asked.

She was youngish. Maybe in her late twenties. Purple hair. Caring eyes.

"What's your name?"

"Thea..." she choked, her tears catching her voice. "My name is Thea..."

"Thea, are you okay?"

"No..."

She wiped tears from her face, though it could have been rainwater, she wasn't sure.

"Come to us, Thea. We'll help you."

She looked at the woman. Searched for where she was. Looked into her home.

Then she was gone.

Thea lost her.

20

It hit April in the chest like a ten-ton weight to the heart.

She collapsed on the carpet and coughed and coughed.

Oscar was at her side. She couldn't see him, but she could feel his hand on her back, catch his outline in the corner of her eye.

"April," he said. "Are you okay?"

This was something like she'd never seen.

As a conduit, she was used to channelling the dead, but she rarely channelled the living – yet she could tell immediately that this was a person awake and with a soul. The energy this person had was overwhelming.

And as soon as she found access to that energy, she understood without any further thought who this person was and why they had suddenly entered her life.

Their gift was such that she could reach into the soul of another Sensitive and grasp it in her hand. April had to do all she could to hold onto her own mind and not have it ripped away, as she did all she could to hold onto this girl and help her as best she could.

"Are you okay?" she asked.

This girl's face. She was young. A teenager. Almost an adult. Wet.

But it wasn't her exterior that troubled April. It was the girl's emotional energy that was holding onto April. This girl was in torment, writhing between this world and the next, riding along a wave of terror until something ripped her apart – whether it was her own uncontrolled ability or something that saw that ability and used it to hurt her.

This girl needed April's help. She had to stay calm. And she had to stay in control – as hard as it was against something so powerful.

"What's your name?" April asked. Maybe if she had a name, she could search for this girl.

"Thea... My name is Thea..." the words were heavy, like through water, but she heard them clearly.

"Thea, are you okay?"

"No..."

Oh, God, this girl... This poor, poor girl...

"Come to us, Thea," April urged. "We'll help you."

She felt her grip loosen.

She tried to hold on, but this girl was too distraught, too conflicted – something within her was losing, something was struggling to hold on.

And, with that final slip of her fingertips, April felt the girl fall away.

She opened her eyes to find Oscar above her, shouting something, probably her name, but she couldn't tell. Julian was there too. So were Maddie and Seb. Watching on at the far end of the room.

"April!" Oscar's voice grew clearer. "April, come on!"

Oscar's lips met hers, but not in a romantic way.

It was at this point she realised he was administering CPR, or at least, as much as he knew of it.

A sudden breath scraped her mouth and she found herself wheezing for more.

It was at this point she realised that she'd stopped breathing.

"Oh my God..." April gasped.

Oscar collapsed on the side of the sofa. He was sweating. Tears had accumulated in the corners of his eyes.

How far had she slipped?

"What – what happened?" April asked, though she already knew the answer.

"You fell, you stopped breathing."

She realised Julian was on the phone. He hung up.

"The ambulance is on its way," he told her.

April shook her head. "I don't need it."

She tried moving, and Oscar grabbed her arm to balance her, guiding her to the sofa.

"I think you do," Oscar told her. "You just collapsed, stopping breathing; that doesn't just happen."

"It didn't just happen," April told him. "It was a vision... No, not a vision, it was real... It was... A girl..."

"You're not making any sense," Julian told her.

She looked up to him and realised he was right. He was so right.

"It's like you said," she told him.

"What do you mean, like I said? What did I say?"

"You said there could be a Sensitive, with the balance... That had been..." Her words weren't forming, but they knew what she was referring to.

"What, you saw her?" Oscar asked, on his knees, holding her hand, looking so concerned.

"Yes, yes, I saw her," she said.

"Go get her a glass of water," Julian barked at the other two, and Maddie scampered out.

"I saw her... Her name, it's Thea... My God, she's..."

"What?" Oscar exclaimed. "She's what?"

"She's so scared... So, so scared..." She turned her face to Oscar, her eyes widening farther than he'd ever seen them widen. "And she is in so much trouble."

April collapsed, and they could do nothing more than put her on her side and wait for the ambulance to arrive.

21

St. Helen's Psychiatric Unit was a hive of chaos. Exhausted nurses and weary doctors drained of energy, pulling longer shifts to support their colleagues, helping each other to hopelessly wrestle manic patients into their rooms.

Elijah ran through the corridor, wiping sweat from his brow, rushing to another nurse's aid. As he did, one of his colleagues ran past him toward the exit.

"Where are you going?" he asked. If they were all facing this, they were facing it together.

"We're out of restraints. I'm going out to see what I can find," she told him as quickly as she could and disappeared down the corridor.

Elijah's gaze lingered momentarily at her path as he let those words sink in.

"Fuck..." he muttered.

He wasn't sure how much of this he could do anymore. He glanced at his watch. It was gone 3.00a.m. His mind was too tired to even work out how long he'd been there. He blinked out the fatigue, unable to force the dryness from his eyes.

His beeper went manic again.

With a reluctant sigh, he continued running to room number...what was it again?

Jesus. There had been so many rooms he'd been called to, he was now unable to even remember a particular number.

He glanced at the number on his beeper – Room 34.

He skidded around the corner and found his way to the open door. Inside the room were three nurses and a doctor doing all they could to pin down a patient, and having very little luck.

"Elijah, get in here!" the doctor demanded.

Elijah rushed in and joined them, pushing down on the patient's chest. It was a woman, at least eighty – but that didn't stop her having strength superior to all of them. She almost managed to leap from the bed, but one of the nurses grabbed her at the very last moment.

Another nurse appeared at the door with some rope.

"This is the best I've got!" the nurse shouted, and ran to the patient's wrists.

"Are you crazy?" Elijah gasped. "This is a human being!"

"We have no more restraints," the doctor summarised. "What do you suggest?"

Elijah went to answer but couldn't. These were extraordinary circumstances. Perhaps they were planning on dealing with the human rights violations at a later point. For now, safety at whatever cost was the priority – for both staff and patients.

He unwillingly accepted the reality of the situation and helped hold the patient's arms down as the nurse haphazardly bound the patient's wrists to the bar of the bed.

"*You...*" the old woman said, flapping her tongue at Elijah. "*You fucking heathen...*"

Her face was empty of anything human. Cracked and

bruised, her skin was falling, her eyes fully dilated, her voice deep and croaky.

"Elijah, focus!" the doctor shouted, and Elijah strengthened his grip.

"Why don't you suck my fucking cunt!" the darling old pensioner asked.

Elijah had heard a lot of things from a lot of patients over the years – but a woman her age making such a request whilst violently slashing her tongue and splashing dollops of drool on her gown was an image he knew was burnt into his memory forever.

The nurse did the other wrist, and as soon as the final knot was tied, they all stood back and watched as the woman writhed and wriggled and thrashed and kicked, never a moment of peace taking over her seizing body.

Elijah closed his eyes, keeping them closed for longer than he could afford himself, then opened them.

"When was the last time you slept?" the doctor asked.

"I don't know," Elijah honestly replied, and tried to remember. "Perhaps, thirty-eight hours ago."

"You need to go sleep," the doctor instructed.

"Can I really afford to?"

"You can't afford not to. We need to take care of our nurses as well. Use the on-call room. Even if just for an hour, you look exhausted."

"I am exhausted."

"Then go."

"How can I, Doctor? Have you seen this place?"

Each of the nurse's beepers came together in a senseless crescendo and they each ran from the room in a mad dash.

"Tell you what," the doctor compromised. "Help us by going to the basement and getting us some more rope. Then rest."

"Oh, no..." Elijah would rather work another thirty-eight hours than do that. "I'd really rather not."

"Please," the doctor said, his beeper going off too. "I'll be in Room 66."

Before Elijah could object, the doctor ran out of the room and around the corner.

The basement was the last place Elijah wanted to go.

EACH WOODEN STEP RESPONDED WITH AN UNSETTLING CREAK, each with a different groan. Some held their elongated, low-pitched response, whilst some just gave an obtuse squelch.

Elijah touched the bottom step and reached out for the light switch, refusing to place a foot on the ground before he'd graced the room with light.

The minute the hazy, artificial hum vaguely illuminated the dank box, the door at the top of the stairs slammed shut.

Elijah convinced himself it was the wind.

Even though there was no wind.

Still, someone could have barged into it. Or it could have swung on its own weight. Or... Or...

I don't know.

Hell, maybe he imagined it. He was exhausted. Maybe his mind was showing him things that weren't there.

The top step creaked.

He looked at it, not sure if it was real, but sure enough, the next step creaked, and the next, and the next.

He shook his head. A tired mind hearing tired things. He stepped into the basement, looking around at all the boxes stacked against the walls, all the unused furniture, mattresses with dead springs, shelves with dusty relics. The pointless light only lit the centre of the room, and all the items gathered around the edges were cast in shadow.

There was no indication as to where the rope was stored.

He stepped deeper into the room, the moisture clinging to his skin, the distant drip providing a metronome to the silence.

Drip. Drip. Drip. Drip. Drip.

Normally, he would find it irritating, but in this situation, he somehow found it comforting. He could pretend it was someone in there with him, keeping him company, watching as he walked further in.

Drip. Drip. Drip. Drip. Drip.

He left the sanctity of the light behind, edging further in. A bunch of boxes were hidden behind a shelf, storing random artefacts such as paint, old stethoscopes, and aged medical books. He made his way behind one of the shelves and took out a box, the damp cardboard bending under his grip.

Drip. Drip. Drip. Drip. Drip.

He dug his hands in, pulling objects aside, wondering why such old, useless items were being stored. Ignoring more creaks of the steps, he persisted to rustling through screwed-up bits of paper and stacks of mangled paper cups.

...

He lifted his head.

Something had changed.

...

The drip. It had stopped.

He peered toward the source of the drip, trying to see where it had come from, as if he'd be able to see the lack of water in the darkness.

Something brushed his shoulder.

He turned his head, as if he could feel someone watching

him. Like someone else was in there with him. Like they'd walked down the stairs, stepped through the basement, and...

The lights went out.

Not in a sudden crack of a light bulb or the smash of a power cut – he heard the click of the light switch and was cast in darkness.

Oh fuck...

He decided he'd get out of the basement, leave as quickly as he could – then realised he had no way of knowing where the steps were. It was complete darkness. There were no windows, no luminous objects – hell, light didn't even come under the crack of the door atop the steps he so desperately wished he could seek out.

He tried walking forward but hit his kneecap on what he assumed was the shelf, instinctively grabbing it as if that would reduce the pain at all.

He stopped moving. Listened carefully.

Light steps, like barefoot on wood, came toward him – the noise so tender that he wasn't sure he'd hear it if he moved at all.

"Hello?" he tried.

The steps ceased.

He remained still, poised in a stand-off with what was probably just a figment of his imagination.

"Is someone there?" he tried again.

No one answered.

What did he expect?

His tired mind was attaching actions to unconnected sounds.

The steps could have been a drip. A tap of water on wood. The shuffle of plastic decompressing.

In all likelihood, it was probably just his awake-for-thirty-eight-hours mind telling him to go to sleep.

Yet, he didn't believe himself.

"Hello?" he tried again and listened.

Really listened.

Peered intently into the black, trying to make out something across the wind.

"Hello," whispered a voice over his shoulder.

He leapt forward, stumbling over boxes and knocking the shelf over. He didn't care. He used the shelf as a guide to find his way to the wall, placed his hands on the cold brick and guided himself to the stairs. He reached the top step, opened the door, slammed it behind him, and didn't stop running until he'd made it up another three flights of stairs and was safely away from whatever was in that Godforsaken basement.

APRIL'S RECOVERY WAS SO SEAMLESS SHE WASN'T SURE WHETHER the doctors believed that she had stopped breathing at all. Sitting in the hospital bed, being told that she seemed absolutely fine and they were going to let her go that afternoon following some final checks, she knew they were just doing it to cover themselves in case of the small possibility that she was being truthful.

But April knew the truth. Being a conduit meant she would, every now and then, find herself channelling something that would feed off her life.

She was in control of her abilities, and it had been a long time since she had allowed something to channel through her without her permission. She was always in control, but what had taken her over was bigger than her – but, despite its overwhelming power, she was lucky; it wasn't evil.

Making sure she was okay, and after April insisting that she was fine for the twelfth time, Oscar left with Julian and Seb. They had to look into who this Thea girl could be, where she could be, and how they could help her. If she was what they thought she could be, then they were lucky – but they still had to find her.

April had, however, asked for Maddie to stay behind. Now, there they were, the two of them sharing comfortable silence as Maddie sat by her side.

"How are you?" April asked.

"Shouldn't I be asking you that?" Maddie replied.

April smiled.

"I still don't understand what actually happened," Maddie said. April could see that Maddie's concern was for sharing the gift – she was worried the same thing could happen to her. And it probably would.

"You don't need to worry," April assured her. "If it ever happens, you are in the best place, surrounded by people who know how to help. We'd bring you right back."

"I don't even get what a conduit even is."

"A conduit," April explained, smiling, warming to this girl, "is someone who channels the spirit of others. Usually, the dead. Occasionally, a demon, if the risk is worth it and people are ready to pull you back. And, just this once, a person."

"But…" Maddie began, then decided not to speak. She didn't need to.

"You're scared?" April observed.

"Yes."

"Because you don't like the idea of something being part of you, sharing your body."

"Yes. Especially something dead, or evil."

April nodded her understanding as she considered her response.

"I can understand that. It's hard to come to terms with. Our bodies and our minds are private – it's something we don't want to share, particularly with something we don't know, something so dangerous."

"Exactly!"

"I felt like that a lot. Then I saw Oscar and Julian. I saw them mid-exorcism, fighting demon after demon, each one wearing down another part of their soul. And do you know what I thought?"

"What?"

"My job is just to have a conversation with something. Their job is to be on the front line, fighting it. I know which one I think is really safer."

Maddie forced a sad smile. April could see her agreement, could see Maddie coming to terms with what she could do, what she had to do.

At times, April forgot Maddie was still just sixteen. A year younger than April was when she began to harness her gift. Those familiar feelings of terror crept up on her, those feelings of mortifying reluctance at embracing what she could do, reminding her exactly how this girl was feeling.

Then again, she also remembered a feeling of happiness that she had finally found a purpose, finally found something she could do, a way she could contribute to the world.

"Do you know why I really asked for you to stay behind?" April asked.

"Why?"

"Because you can feel it, can't you?"

"What? Feel what?"

"*Him.*"

"Who's *him?*"

April looked around herself.

"He's here in the room with us, isn't he?"

Maddie's face went from grateful recognition to turgid fear. As if she was glad that April felt it too, then terrified that it was real.

"Who is he?" Maddie asked.

"Oh, no one evil. Nothing bad. Just a man who once had this bed. A man who is struggling to let go of it."

"Like – a man who's dead?"

"Yes. Precisely. What kind of man do you think he is?"

"I don't know."

"Close your eyes. Listen. Feel. Then tell me."

Maddie closed her eyes. April studied her carefully, her youthful skin wrinkling in the tight scrunch of her eyelids. Her head flickering with concentration.

After a few minutes, she opened her eyes.

"I think he's in his eighties. Maybe, eighty-seven. I think his name is Brian."

April grinned. Damn, this girl had talent.

"Wow," April said. "Well done."

"You mean – you mean I got it right?"

"Well, it's what I picked up on."

Maddie beamed.

"So what do we do now?" she asked.

April took Maddie's hand in hers.

"We talk to him."

24

MADDIE ENTERED SERIOUS MODE WITH A RAPIDITY NOT MANY people could rival. Not that she was being particularly unserious, but she had been relaxed.

Not anymore.

She leant forward in her chair, listening carefully to every word April said and repeating back every instruction.

Maddie is never to do this alone, by herself.

Maddie is never to willingly let a spirit enter her body until she has learnt how to control it.

Maddie is always to keep hold of April's hand.

April will only do this without Oscar and Julian nearby because they know the spirit means no harm – but if anything goes wrong, she is to contact Oscar immediately.

Maddie is to be the one who talks to the spirit.

And, despite the grave worries she had about this gift, it was that final instruction that scared her most.

She was to talk to the man. The man in April's body. She was to talk to him and convince him to move on.

Maddie wasn't a big talker. She could easily go through a school day saying nothing more than *yes miss* to the register and *thanks* to the teacher handing out a worksheet. If someone spoke to her, she would find herself retreating in on herself, covering her face, answering in single words with minimal syllables – then afterwards, she would hate herself for being so rude and rejecting any potential friends.

But she was entering a new world now. And she trusted April.

It was time to be the person they all kept telling her she was going to be.

Only, she wished she could believe in that person as much as they all did.

"Are you ready?" April checked, perching on the edge of the bed.

Maddie gave a disjointed nod, though she wasn't sure she'd ever be ready.

"Take my hand."

Maddie did as she was told.

"Hold onto it tight. Your grip on my hand could be my grip on this world. No matter what this man does or says, do not let go of it."

"I won't."

She decided to grip April's hand with both of hers, just to make sure.

April closed her eyes.

Maddie studied her carefully.

At first, it just looked as if April was going to sleep. She was so still, Maddie had to watch her chest carefully to see that it was still rising.

April stayed like this for a while, still and peaceful. Maddie watched her, ready, waiting, but started to wonder if this was going to work.

Just as she wondered it, April sniffed. But it wasn't a gentle sniff, it was a manly sniff – big, and lurching her head to the side.

She opened her eyes, but her eyes weren't hers. She looked vulnerable – rather, *he* looked vulnerable. The features were still April's, but they moved in a different way. The brow was lower, the mouth was smaller, the nose curled up.

He looked around himself, then down at her body.

"What – where am I?" he stuttered.

It was like April's voice, but a pitch she wouldn't speak at. Lower, like a man's, but the high pitch of a man in a fight with anxiety.

"What is this? What's happened to my body?"

Maddie went to speak, but only formed a few abject syllables. What was she supposed to say?

"What are you doing to me?"

Maddie couldn't find the response. She willed herself to say something, but didn't.

Come on... she urged herself.

"What are you doing to me!" he repeated, but in a desperate cry.

Sensing the anger growing in the man's voice, Maddie forced herself to speak.

"Hello, Brian," she said. "My name is Maddie."

"What? Who are you? How do you know my name?" He looked down. "Let go of my hand!"

"I – well – I, erm, I'm afraid I can't do that, Brian."

"What? Why do you keep saying my name? I don't know you!"

"Do you know this room?" she tried, an attempt to bring back familiarity.

He looked around himself.

"Yes. This is my hospital room."

"Why are you here?"

"Why, that's none of your business!"

"I'm just trying to help you, Brian."

"You don't look like a nurse."

"No, Brian, I'm not. I'm a–" she thought about saying it, then did so with a grin. "I'm a Sensitive."

"A Sensitive? What is that?"

"It means I can speak to dead people, Brian.""Dead people? You're crazy!"

"Look around yourself. Look at your body. Does this seem right?"

He looked down at April's body. He sobbed, tears dampening April's cheeks.

"What is this…"

"You had cancer, Brian," she told him, impressing herself by being able to pick up on his illness. She then felt guilty that she was pleased about this, and felt bad for him having such a horrific illness.

"Yes, I know!"

"But you don't anymore. Do you know why?"

"I – I'm cured?"

"No, Brian. You're dead. It killed you. I'm so sorry."

He looked back at her, his eyes lingering on her stare, her face a mix of shock and humility. He seemed offended by her, by her rudeness, her forthrightness, and her downright lies.

"I do not find this funny," he spat. "Fetch me a doctor."

Maddie gently shook her head, trying to be as firm yet reassuring as she could be.

"No, Brian. There's no doctor coming. Not now."

He shook his head with more and more vigour. "No. No – you – you belong in the nuthouse."

"Brian, please. You're in a woman's body, she is channelling your spirit. You've been dead a while. Think about it, you must know this is true."

He glared at her. A glare that morphed into sadness, an aching sadness that clung to his face and wouldn't go away. She felt so bad for him – it must be horrific, to learn that your life is over and all your loved ones are still here as you have to move on.

"But – my wife. Where is my wife?"

"Tell me about your wife, Brian."

"Oh, my wife. She's incredible. Eighty-six and still walking on her own two feet."

"Sounds like you two have had quite the life together."

"Married since I was twenty-two. Forty-five years."

"Wow, that's quite a while."

Brian's sobs increased, and Maddie had to quell her own tears. She had to stop talking about his wife, stop talking about things that would keep him on this Earth. She wanted to know about his children, but she knew that would only make him more attached, so she didn't.

"Your wife will join you when she's ready, Brian."

"No… No, I can't leave her…"

"Do you really want her to see you like this?"

He looked down at April's body. "No."

"You can wait for her. Wear your best suit, comb your hair back, get some flowers. However many years she takes, eventually, she will find you. I promise."

He placed April's second hand on top of hers and held tightly, squeezing. He nodded, wiping tears on April's shoulder.

"Are you ready, Brian?" Maddie asked.

He gazed at her. His eyes turning from despairing denial to despairing acceptance. Reluctantly, he nodded.

"It's time," she told him.

"God bless you," he said to her, ever so softly. "God bless you, Maddie. Thank you."

She smiled.

With a final smile in return, April's eyes closed and her body, whilst still remaining upright, flopped.

Maddie watched her, wondering how long it would take for her to return.

April's eyes remained closed. The tick of the clock in the corner created a beat to Maddie's patience. She had no idea how long it took for April to come back around, but it didn't matter – she would wait.

Maddie looked down. Thought about what she'd just done. She felt good about helping him, but sad for his life lost.

Still, it sounded like he'd had a long life, full of love.

"You were incredible," April said.

Maddie abruptly lifted her head to find April's drooping eyes smiling back at her.

"Thanks."

"No, really. You did so well. I'm so proud of you."

They sat together until the doctor returned and gave April the all-clear to leave. The whole time, Maddie remained silent, thinking about Brian's wife and hoping that, wherever she was, she was okay.

25

THE ANSWER MACHINE IN OSCAR AND APRIL'S KITCHEN HADN'T stopped blinking for the last few weeks. They'd resorted to recording a message that said they weren't currently taking on any new cases due to overwhelming workload, yet they still came in. Mothers, fathers, sons, grandmothers, dear friends – all pleading with them to just take this one case, just to help their loved one before things became any worse.

Honestly, their work was no longer being dictated by clients, but by the Vatican. The need for action on a bigger scale kept growing and growing, a shadow hanging over their shoulders, forever looming, every day another inch.

But, on this particular occasion, when the phone began to ring again, April's head lifted from her coffee. Oscar was still fussing over her, still asking her what she needed, whether she was okay, whilst Julian just sat silently opposite her.

April, however, felt the relevance of this call in the pit of her stomach, and she welcomed the opportunity for everyone to stop forcing constant care upon her.

"Take the call," she blankly instructed.

"What?" Oscar asked, perplexed. "The answer machine will get it, there's no need–"

"Take it."

Reluctantly, Oscar lifted the phone and answered it with a cautious, "Hello?"

He left the room to speak, leaving April alone with Julian. A silence fell between them like one they'd never had. Awkwardness had never featured in their relationship, nor had discomfort. They had been close since the day they'd met; Julian like an older brother, giving her all the guidance she needed to change her life. But now, there seemed to have been a shift – since that argument a few days ago, they hadn't exchanged a meaningful conversation, and the growing unease became sickly pertinent.

"How are you?" Julian asked.

"Fine," April answered.

"I know Oscar keeps trying to pander to you, but the kid just thinks you're–"

"So you're defending him now?"

Julian looked down at his drink. He'd rejected a coffee, instead opting for whiskey. He sipped it, relishing the sharp sting, and held the glass by his lips to quell the discomfort.

"I'm just saying," Julian said.

"Oh yeah. What are you just saying?"

"April, please, I–"

The door opened and Oscar walked in. His face had fallen to a look of concern, something that told April he was right to take the call.

"It, er… It's St. Helen's Psychiatric Unit."

Their heads fell. They had already failed there, and they didn't welcome the prospect of going again.

"A guy called Elijah, one of the mental health nurses. Says it's pandemonium. That patients are attacking other patients."

"Well, of course they are," Julian piped up. "Imagine that much demonic influence in one place."

A moment of silence fell as they all dreaded the words Julian was about to speak – dreaded them, as they knew it themselves.

"We need to go back."

"But we've already been there," Oscar said. "It didn't work."

"We can't abandon it."

As much as April could see Oscar hated it, he knew Julian was right.

"This guy, Elijah, he says it's worse in the basement. Maybe that could be the place to start."

They sat back and contemplated this.

"Let's go down there," April suggested. "Away from whatever's going on above – if we're so worried about this place and the patients in it, maybe that would be the best place to start. I'll see what I can channel–"

"No," Oscar interrupted, determinedly shaking his head.

"Oscar, I'm fine."

"You stopped breathing, April."

"I often stop breathing when I channel something bad. That's why you're there – to get rid of it if need be."

"I don't like the idea, I think it's–"

"All Seb and Maddie have witnessed is us failing, and failing catastrophically," April pointed out. "The only way for us to restore that faith is to put ourselves on the line to show them we are not afraid."

"I don't think risking your life to make a point is a good idea."

"I think risking our lives is what we're going to be doing every day now. Besides, I'm not risking anything we haven't risked a hundred times before."

"But it's different now."

"It's the same, it's just the quantity that's changed."

"I still don't like it."

April looked to Julian.

"We'll be there," he said to Oscar. "We'll keep her safe."

Only April could see how difficult it was for Julian to say something reassuring to Oscar, and she was grateful for it.

"Do you honestly not think it's a risk?" Oscar said, his face looking a lot less convinced than his words.

April shook her head.

"Not at all," she told him.

Oscar ran his hands through his hair, exhaled heavily. She could see how difficult he was finding this. But, to an extent, Julian was right – this was bigger than them, and they had to start making decisions accordingly.

"It's not a risk, Oscar. We know what we're doing," she said.

"Fine. I'll tell the others. Let's leave in an hour."

He left.

April turned to Julian.

"Thanks," she said quietly.

With a slight nod, he stood up and got himself ready for the fight.

26

It was like having a map, but with no light to shine on it. Thea could feel it in her hands, but had no way of seeing the direction.

Like there was a guiding light, but too out of focus and too high in the sky for her to quite make out its instructions.

She had felt it. The woman. April. She had seen her, spoken to her, and she'd said she could help.

She knew where they were, but she didn't.

She had a direction, she just didn't have instructions.

She had to rely on instinct, on gut alone.

She had to think, despite the so many, many voices shouting at her. She wasn't even sure what were her own thoughts anymore. Was it her arguing with herself, or was it something telling her they needed help or that she was doomed?

She kept running.

Running out of town, running past the voices, past the faces, past the claws, the fangs, the pale skin, the rotting flesh, the gaping wounds – past all of it, until she reached a forest, and she searched through the trees and found a field.

A field, where she was all alone.

For a moment, clarity settled in. They had gone. It was the eye of the storm, a moment of peace where her mind could make sense of her emotions.

But it didn't last long.

She looked up and they surrounded her. Walking through the field, over the bushes, wading through the weeds to get toward her. So many grave faces, reaching hands, begs, pleads, threats.

So many of them.

She knew where to go, she just had to realise it.

She kept walking.

Closing her eyes, she prayed for focus that never arrived.

She had to follow the way, had to find them, had to get to them.

She had to.

Somehow, she had to.

THEN

DEREK WATCHED JULIAN, AS HE OFTEN DID ON QUIET EVENINGS when they had little to do. Sat in his garden, a book on his lap and a sherry in his hand, he'd get distracted from the words he held and raise his eyes to Julian.

At this particular moment, Julian was sat on the bench across the garden, his eyes closed and his head rested on his fist.

It had been a long day. Derek wasn't surprised Julian was sleeping.

Another exorcism, another successful battle, but another piece of your soul cracked at. He could see it in Julian, just as he once saw it in Eddie and saw it in himself. With every demon they defeated there had been another part of themselves they'd lost, another part that burnt and smoked away.

Derek wasn't sure how much of himself he had left. But Julian, who was still so young – he had so much of himself left, Derek was unsure whether it was fair to direct him into this battle.

Then again, if people weren't around to fight these battles, people would die.

It was an unfair trade.

A point that, when he finally came face-to-face with his Maker, he would be raising.

He had other concerns for Julian, however.

He was reckless.

Foolish.

Quick to jump to decisions and opinions and slow to challenge his own thoughts.

Derek wasn't going to be around forever. Julian was going to be his legacy. Julian was going to be the one who finished what Derek was starting: recruiting, training, guiding.

Could Julian guide anyone?

The kid could barely guide himself.

Then again, isn't that how everyone starts?

Once upon a time, he didn't even believe in any of this. It took a drastic experience for him to believe. His changed beliefs alienated his fiancée and she left, but he never debated whether it was the right decision to let her go and carry on with the life he was leading.

Should he have?

Should he have fought for her?

Thought more?

No. He was just doubting himself because he felt doubting himself was what he should do. He regretted nothing.

He doubted that Julian would get to his age and regret nothing.

Julian shifted places and the book that perched on his lap, one Derek had instructed him to read in order to help him familiarise himself with demonology folklore, fell from Julian's lap to the dirty tufts of grass beneath. It was an old book, but Derek stopped himself from being cross. Julian didn't value what was old and sacred like he did.

But he would.

One day.

Hopefully.

Would he be able to lead like Derek foresaw? Would Julian be able to quell that thoughtless impatience he exuded in such great quantities?

Derek closed his eyes.

Maybe, maybe not.

For now, it was time for his thoughts to quieten.

Time for peace in his mind.

Julian would grow.

He would learn not to be so ruthless, so intolerant, or so hasty in his anger.

Derek was sure of it.

He was like Julian once.

He was.

We all were.

And Derek was sure of it.

He really was.

NOW

28

A SENSE OF FOREBODING CAME OVER OSCAR. IT STARTED IN HIS gut, spreading through to his stomach where it twisted him into sickness, punched his heart into pounding before lurching up through his throat in a mouthful of sick that he immediately swallowed.

He looked at the others as they stepped out of the car. Julian with his dogged, determined, never-show-a-smile-when-you-can-show-a-frown face was on – whether this was his difficult face or his game face, Oscar was yet to know.

Following them was Seb and Maddie, still so young, so unaware – still yet to have any genuine experience in honing their skills. Seb strutting like he owned the car he stepped out of and the ground he stepped upon, hiding whatever deeper levels were beneath his smooth façade – Oscar was unsure whether he was certain those deeper levels were there, or whether he was just hoping. Maddie trailed behind him, the complete opposite, shuffling her body forward, never looking anyone in the eyes.

Then, behind them, the ever-present backbone of the task, April. That same smile on her face that gave him goose pimples the first time he saw her and still gave him goose pimples now. He was so lucky, he knew that. The thing he loved most about April – and the thing he also found most frustrating – was that she didn't need him. She wasn't in need of a man to support her – she loved him by choice. Being a strong, independent woman meant that she believed in her choices, whether right or wrong – and although weaker men would see this as unattractive stubbornness, Oscar saw it as power.

But he had this sickly feeling, a worry that this power was going to be her downfall.

He realised this worry was for her. For what they were about to do, in a place that had been the only fight they had fled from.

"We shouldn't be doing this," he stated.

Julian shrugged and made his way through the gates and up the path to the door, followed by Maddie and Seb.

Oscar stopped April, taking her hands, holding them tightly.

"April, we can still back out. We can just go home now, figure it out, think it over. It's not too late."

Her eyes smiled as she placed her soft hand against his cheek.

"Oscar, I love you so much," she told him. "But everything we do now is a risk. We will risk each other, and we will risk the world. We have to be brave."

"Yes, I agree we have to be brave, but this–"

"Oscar, it's just a routine process. We're not attempting to exorcise anyone, we're just going to the basement and seeing what we find."

"What then? What about when we have to face the rest? There are more than we can exorcise, even us."

"Oscar – do you trust me?"

"Yes, of course."

He said those three dreaded words before he had time to

consider their implications. She said nothing more, knowing that this would be enough.

He did trust her.

He just...

She took his hand and led him up the path, where Julian had already made contact with Elijah.

"It's pandemonium in there," Elijah was saying. "Every one of them is going crazy, being pinned down. Sedatives aren't even working on them. We're just having to do what we can to protect ourselves."

"We know what the situation is," Julian said. "It's..." He glanced over his shoulder at Oscar. "...It's something we're working on."

"I – I just – I've never seen anything like this."

"You said something about the basement?"

"Uh huh, it was freaky. It was like...like, there was something down there, with me."

"Can you take us there?" April requested, and Elijah gave a nod, a less than enthused nod, one that Oscar might give when being asked to get rid of a spider. Something he knew he shouldn't have any difficulty with – but something that terrified him nonetheless.

Elijah led them through the corridors, and they were immediately hit by a salvo of screams. Oscar flinched away at the piercing shouts, the growls, the bombardment of agony. A glance at the others showed that they were struggling against it too – but Elijah just walked like he had become accustomed to it.

Eventually, he reached the door to the basement and held his hand out to it.

"I'm not going down there," he declared.

"You can wait for us up here," Julian said, opening the door and leading the way down the steps.

Aesthetically, it was the same as every other basement –

cardboard boxes, damp, drips, moisture on the air, a poor light illuminating little but a circle beneath it.

But they all felt it. As soon as they all stood, silently engaging the mood, they all knew they weren't alone.

"Are you ready?" Julian asked April, Oscar pleading that she would say no.

"I'll do it," came an unexpectedly bold voice behind them.

They all turned and looked at Maddie.

"I want to do it. Let me."

29

"ARE YOU CRAZY?" OSCAR DEMANDED OF APRIL, HAVING TAKEN her aside to the far corner of the basement, which did little to hide their conversation.

"I am not crazy."

"She's a kid! She hasn't done one before, she doesn't know what she's doing."

"But I do!"

"How does that change anything?"

"I'll be with her throughout it all. I'll guide her."

"Can't you feel it? What's in here? It's too strong, it's a bad idea."

"I am not a kid," Maddie spoke up. "And I *can* do this."

Oscar hesitated. He appreciated her gumption, but now was not the time.

"Look, Maddie, I know you mean well–"

"Meaning well will do nothing against what we're fighting," Maddie said. "I hear you all talking at night. I know what it is we're up against, I'm not stupid. And I know we have less than a year until it becomes permanent."

"Then you know why it's such a reckless idea."

"But if you're involving me in the fight, I'm going to need to know what I'm doing. And that means throwing me in at the deep end if you have to."

Oscar shook his head, but before he could argue further, Julian turned to him, his face a blank mess.

"She's right," Julian said. "We haven't long, and she needs to learn. She'll only do that by experiencing it."

"*Now* you speak up," Oscar said, glaring at Julian. "*Now* you decide to contribute something."

"If she feels up to it, then let her. We'll all be here, we can bring her back if it goes wrong."

Oscar looked back at April, looking back at him with that same face she always had when he knew he was about to lose an argument. He felt slightly betrayed, annoyed that April's opinion aligned with Julian's – but he was outnumbered. What could he do?

"Fine." He threw his arms helplessly into the air. "Fine, but I'm not going to be a part of it. It's your grave you're digging."

Oscar walked away from the centre of the room to the far wall, where he leant with his arms folded.

April stepped forward, but before she moved completely away from Oscar, she reached a hand out and squeezed his.

"Thank you," she said, so quietly only he would hear it.

She stood in the centre of the room, waving Maddie toward her. Julian stood beside them, and Seb stood out of the way, on the far side of the room to Oscar.

April put her hands around Maddie's face, looking into those determined eyes, that youthful face so full of promise. She was going to be brilliant, she could tell. Maybe even better than April.

"Are you ready?" April asked.

Maddie nodded.

"Just listen to me, and do everything I say. Okay?"

"I will."

"Okay, close your eyes."

Maddie closed her eyes.

"Now listen. Listen to everything – to the room, to the feet on the surface, the drips. Listen to it. Let it mix with your mind so it becomes part of your thoughts, so it becomes part of you."

Oscar held his breath.

A box shuffled behind him.

A shadow moved past Seb's shoulder.

Something was already here.

He stood, tensing his arms. He shovelled a hand into his pocket where his crucifix was and grabbed it, ready to do battle if need be.

"Now zoom in," April continued. "Zoom in on the sounds, to things you wouldn't normally hear, to the air. Take in the smells, take in the feeling, the mood of what's here."

Maddie's eyelids flickered.

It was working.

Something pushed Oscar.

"Okay, now listen to it. Listen to it, and tell us what it has to say."

He could see it, encircling Maddie. Its face in the smoke of the light, its claws gripping her neck.

And he knew very well in that moment that everything was about to go wrong.

30

Maddie could feel the spirit grip her.

It was behind her. Before her. Above her, below her – *inside her.*

She could feel the spirit spread through her body, through her mind.

She could feel the spirit until she realised it wasn't a spirit.

Until she realised she'd made a very bad mistake.

It was angry. Furious. Beyond furious – it was livid, wrathful, but also cocky. Pleased that she'd opened herself up to it, pleased that she'd foolishly let it in.

Oh, little Madison...

She moved her head around the room, looking for the voice, though her eyes wouldn't open.

They wouldn't open.

Why wouldn't they open?

Red.

A flicker of blood red.

Then her eyes opened, but she saw nothing. Her pupils were facing somewhere inside and, although she could feel the room on her eyes, she could see nothing.

She heard screaming. It sounded like Oscar's screaming, or Julian, or Seb, and April was in there somewhere, but it was far away, distant, like it was in a house next to hers.

So full of promise... Thinking you can take on the world...

Okay. You can go away now.

It didn't respond.

Please. You can go away now.

It grinned. She couldn't see its grin, but she could feel it, smell it, almost touch it. But its touch was rough, coarse, like scales of a lizard but more prickly.

"Go away!" she screamed.

It cackled. The cackles played on surround sound around her head, from every corner. She turned her head to look for its source, but all she found was red.

Your friends...

"Please!"

I'm going to make you kill them...

"No! No, don't! Go away!"

You let me in, Maddie... You did this...

She tried to hear April's voice, to hear her guidance, to listen to what she was telling Maddie – but the voice was somewhere gone, quelled, inside a box, hidden away; she was being taken over.

You can go away now.

Or you can stay.

No, why did I say that?

Please.

Who am I?

She couldn't even decipher her own thoughts from the entity. It had mixed, amalgamated, confined itself in the synapses of her brain, firing back and forth, she was angry, full of hate, and she wanted to kill her friends, wanted to kill them, she wanted to maim them hurt them eat them fuck them devour them, make them scream scream scream oh God oh God what's happening what am I doing?

She felt her body leap, her claws digging into wood. She swiped at something, possibly Julian, possibly not.

I hate you.

She dove, feeling something collapse under her feet and tried to place her fangs in her neck but something took hold of her took her off took her away and she swiped at them felt blood felt something thick down her arm and

oh God

it won't stop

it keeps going

why

why

why

why

they are going to die because I am going to kill them

why am I killing them?

why am I hurting them?

because they deserve it they think they can win we've already won why

No.

I am Maddie.

I am not a demon.

I am real, and I am still here.

She fought it, swiped her arms but she had nothing to fight, nothing she could punch or hit, it was already there, in her, and it was going to hurt everyone, kill everyone.

She had to stop it.

But how?

How?

how how how how how how how how how how how

"*Aargh!*" she felt her body flex unnaturally backwards as she moaned and groaned and writhed and she knew.

The only way.
It was a part of her now.
She had to end it by ending her.

OSCAR'S SCREAMS AT SEB AND APRIL TO HOLD HER DOWN MADE his throat grow hoarse, made his throat burn, but that didn't matter. It wasn't relevant.

"That You spare us, that You pardon us, that You bring us to true penance, You hear us!" he bellowed in Maddie's face.

"Hear us, O Lord!" Julian faithfully answered.

Oscar felt Julian's crucifix over his shoulder just as he felt his in his own hand, hurting his fingers and palm from the indent of its edges.

Maddie's face turned to him, completely off kilt from her body. Her arms twisted wayward, her legs contorting haphazardly, her body curved backwards into a demented semi-circle.

Her eyes were open, but her pupils weren't there. Just bloodshot white gaping back at him.

"By Your death and burial, by Your holy resurrection, by Your wondrous ascension!"

"Hear us, O Lord!"

"Your Lord doesn't hear you..."

Its voice was a mix of upper and lower inflexions, twisting between the extremes of one pitch to another.

"I have her..."

"By the coming of the Holy Spirit, the Advocate, on the day of judgement!"

"The day of judgement is already here..."

"Hear us, O Lord!"

Oscar appreciated Julian's answering, but he could hear it in his voice – that disbelief. As if they all knew that this wouldn't work. That this demon had already entwined itself with Maddie's body and buried her soul somewhere they couldn't reach.

In a sudden spurt of strength, Maddie's arm hit out and punched Oscar. Oscar collapsed in a heap, grabbing his chin, waiting for the initial pain to die.

Maddie leapt to her feet and jumped over to the shelves, searching for something.

"What's it looking for?" Oscar asked.

"I have no idea."

Oscar held out his crucifix and marched forward.

"God, by Your name, save me, and by Your might, defend my cause."

Without even turning her body, Maddie lifted a hand out – and without this hand even touching Oscar, it sent him across the room.

He took to his feet once again and proceeded forward.

"We all go at once," Oscar said, looking to Julian beside him.

"Where is your crucifix?" Oscar asked of Seb.

Seb withdrew it. His face was not the epitome of cool charm anymore. It was a wreck of terror.

"Hold it tight, and hold it out," Oscar instructed him.

Seb did what he said, though the crucifix shook at the end of his quivering arm.

"God, hear my prayer, hearken to the words of my mouth."

They walked toward her.

She still searched the box, still sought something out.

RICK WOOD

"I will offer you my sacrifice and I will–"

Maddie's face turned toward them.

Her pupils were back. Her face had returned. Her mouth agape.

She had something in her hand. Something she held behind her back.

Oscar lifted his hand and they stopped edging forward. He pointed a reassuring open palm toward her, doing all he could to calm her.

"Maddie, is that you?"

She was crying. Her sniffs accompanied the shake of her head, though Oscar knew this was no demon he was talking to – as much as he knew the demon was still in there.

"Maddie, we are going to try and get this demon out of you, okay?"

She shook her head, vigorously, sniffing more tears away.

"You just have to let us face it, Maddie, okay? You just have to let us–"

"No," she stated.

She took her arm out from behind her back. In her hand was a sharp pair of scissors.

"Maddie, put them down."

"You can't get it out," she sobbed. "You can't. You won't!"

"We've done it plenty of times, I just need you to trust me."

"No. This is the only way."

Oscar looked to April, then to Julian, clueless faces with no idea as to what to do.

"Maddie, please, trust me, you have to trust me. We can do it, you just – you just need to put the scissors down."

"It's too strong for you," Maddie whispered. "You won't do it."

"Maddie, please, I just need you to put them down."

Her hand gripping the scissors began to lower, falling to her side, her hold on the scissors loosening.

144

"That's it, Maddie. That's it."

The scissors hung loosely on the end of a finger.

"Just drop them, Maddie, okay? Just drop them."

She lifted the finger out to let them drop.

In a movement too quick for Oscar to register, her face was overcome once more, her pupils disappearing back into the back of her eyes. A growl and screech forced its way out of her jaw, spewing its ferocity at those gathered around her.

"Grab it!" Julian shouted.

It was too late.

In a swift motion, Maddie's arm had dragged the pointed end of the scissors over her free wrist, then across her throat.

OSCAR DOVE TO MADDIE'S SIDE, IMMEDIATELY APPLYING pressure to her neck.

"Get a doctor!" he screamed. "Now!"

Seb rushed up the steps.

Julian and April found their way to behind Oscar, but he ignored them. He just kept his hand on her throat, kept pressure, kept her alive.

Out the corner of his eye, he saw April kick the scissors away.

"It's okay," Oscar kept telling Maddie. "It's okay, it's okay. It's going to be okay."

But she wasn't responding.

Her body was already limp. The blood had already drenched his trousers, and its pool was expanding slowly, creeping away from him toward the shoes of the others.

Seb rushed back down the steps.

"None of the doctors will come down here," he said.

"Are you kidding?" Oscar shouted.

"They say if you want to get her help, you need to bring her up."

"Tell them she's bleeding out, that she's dying, and that we can't move her!"

"I – I did… They still… They won't… They are all busy, no one will listen…"

"Oscar," Julian said.

Oscar ignored him.

"Come on, Maddie, come on," Oscar urged.

He tried to lift her, but her body had somehow grown heavier, and as he lifted her the neck wound expanded, like it completely came apart. It reminded him of the open mouth of the muppet show he used to watch as a kid, the way the wound opened to such a big space, and he hated himself for thinking it.

"Oscar," came Julian's voice again.

Oscar ignored him.

"Hold on, Maddie, we're going to get you some help, it'll be all right, it'll be all right."

He tried to put more pressure on the wound, but found his hand soaking into it, prodding the exposed muscles of the neck. As he took his hand away, he saw the extremity of the width of the wound, spread across the entire front part of her throat.

He tried to lift her head, to put the wound back together, but it wouldn't fit, like pieces of a puzzle that were meant to go together but didn't.

"Oscar," Julian said.

Oscar ignored him.

"Oscar."

"Fuck off!" Oscar screamed.

Julian crouched beside him and Oscar felt the grip of his hand on his shoulder.

"Oscar, she's already dead," he told her. "The wound's too big. Her neck is ripped open, there's nothing we can do."

"No!"

"Oscar, we can't save her."

Something punched into Oscar's belly.

April was taken off her feet.

Julian resisted a push on his back.

"It's getting angrier, Oscar, it's not safe for us here."

"But if we can just get a doctor–"

"Oscar, we are going."

"Then leave me! Go and leave me!"

Julian tucked his hands beneath Oscar's shoulders and pulled him up. Oscar resisted, trying to kick him off, but Julian held on.

Something flew into them and hit them against the wall.

"It's getting worse, Oscar, come on."

"No! It's our fault! We can't leave, it's our fault!"

He felt a familiar hand inside his, squeezing.

"Oscar..." came April's voice. He caught sight of her face, tears streaming down it.

He got to his feet and walked toward the stairs, pushing against resistance. It felt like he was wading through water.

He looked over his shoulder at the corpse, inside out, messy and incomplete.

He was pushed against the wall.

He put his hand behind April's shoulder and pushed her up the stairs first.

"Now you," Julian instructed.

With the help of Julian grabbing hold of his arm, he made it to the steps.

The next thing he knew, they were in the corridors of St. Helen's Psychiatric Unit, running, covering their ears.

The screams were even louder, accompanied by rattling. Every bed, every door, every loose utensil was battering against walls and floors and anything it could.

Shrieks of nurses and shouts for help were buried beneath it all.

Oscar looked back. He should help. He wanted to help.

A hand, he assumed Julian's, gripped his arm and pulled him away.

Somehow, he found his way to the car. He looked down to find him and the seat beneath him covered in blood.

"What... How..."

April placed her hand on him. Though he didn't feel it, it was enough.

He watched the psychiatric unit disappear in the rear-view mirror, fading until there was nothing left.

THEN

JULIAN WATCHED DEREK IN AWE. ALWAYS SO CALM. HE WAS ONE of those rare people who exuded authority without ever having to appear authoritative. He just stood, spoke to people with a gentle voice, and they bought what he said.

If it was Julian in Derek's situation, he'd be a mess. The trial was to begin the next day, and it was anyone's guess which way it was going to go. A young girl had died during an exorcism, and the verdict would most likely depend on what the jury's beliefs were. If they believed in demons, they would see Derek as a man doing all he could to help the girl – if they didn't, they would see Derek as a deluded, ageing man neglecting the needs of a young girl for a ridiculous purpose.

His stomach gurgled. Julian was getting hungry, but he didn't want to say anything. How selfish would it be of him at this moment to interrupt Derek getting his affairs in order to see if anyone fancied ordering a pizza.

Eventually, Derek dismissed his lawyers and his entourage of people, each performing a function that Julian couldn't identify. He walked over to Julian and looked him up and down.

"I bet you're hungry," said Derek. "Let's eat."

Derek created a dish within ten minutes. A few slices of chicken with some spinach, noodles, and hoi sin sauce – the leftovers of his fridge. Once it was finished and everyone else had left, Derek sat alone with Julian at the table, each of them eating.

Despite being hungry, Julian suddenly felt sick.

"How are you so calm?" Julian asked.

"Why wouldn't I be calm?" Derek answered, though Julian knew he was just being pedantic.

"Come on, Derek."

Derek looked up at Julian and his old eyes made him feel so young, so inexperienced. Which he probably was – but he rarely felt it as much as he did at this moment.

"Let me ask you a question," Derek proposed, placing another spoonful of noodles in his mouth. "Say I wasn't calm. Say I was going crazy. Say I was rushing around here, dancing about, going on about what could happen, growing exceedingly anxious at this and that. What would that accomplish?"

Julian wasn't sure whether he was meant to answer, so he gave a non-committal shrug.

"What's going to happen, will happen," Derek continued. "Whether I choose to be anxious about it or not. So I choose not to be."

"Surely it's not easy to just decide that?"

"Everything's as easy as a decision, Julian. Learn that and your life will become so much easier."

A few minutes passed without anyone speaking. They both finished their food, pushed their dishes aside, and sipped on their glasses of water.

"The real question," Derek said, "is what will happen if I am found guilty."

"Surely you won't be."

"It's a possibility, Julian, and one that we need to be ready for."

"Well then, we appeal, we kick up a fuss, maybe we contact the Vatican."

"No, Julian, I'm not talking about what will happen with my case. I'm talking about what will happen with you. With our mission."

Derek stood, took the dishes to the sink, and put the kettle on. Julian waited quietly, waiting for Derek to finish what he was saying. Once Derek had made them both a coffee and they were settled on two armchairs next to each other in the living room, he spoke once more.

"There are Sensitives everywhere. Awakening. Some with such little gifts they won't notice – but some who are as strong as you."

"And you," Julian pointed out.

"No, not me," Derek chuckled. "I am just a man who knows a lot. I have tried and tried, but you are the one with the innate ability. As will be the rest of the Sensitives. And it's up to you to find them if I'm not there to do it with you."

"But how? How will I find them?"

"It's part of your gift, Julian. Listen for them, and you will find them. Or, heck, some of them may even find you."

Julian nodded, though he still didn't understand how he was supposed to find these people. And, after he'd found them, then what? Was he supposed to train them? Teach them how to hone what they have?

How could he do that when he knew so little himself?

"Confidence," Derek stated, as if knowing what Julian was fretting about, "is an underestimated skill. Arrogance is not the same as confidence; that is confidence with conceit – but confidence will take you anywhere you want to be."

"So I just need to act like I know what I'm doing?" Julian said with an air of preposterousness about the suggestion.

"Precisely," Derek confirmed. "You think I always know what I'm doing?"

"Well, you always seem to."

"Exactly."

"But how will I know? I mean, things, things about demons and what to do; how will I know?"

"In my study, you will find my journals. Use them. They contain the accumulated knowledge of my entire life. They include what happened in The Edward King War." Julian raised his eyebrows – Derek hardly ever talked about this. "They include notions, ideas, suggestions – everything you will need to do what you need to do."

"But, what if…" Julian trailed off.

Derek watched him expectantly. "Yes?"

"What if…I get too scared. I mess it up."

"Then you mess it up. Then, you fix it. It's what we do."

Julian shook his head. "I can't do this alone."

"And you won't. Like I said, either you will find them" – Derek focussed on Julian's eyes with his – "or they will find *you*."

NOW

34

APRIL MADE A COFFEE FOR EVERYONE AND BROUGHT THEM IN ON a tray with a glass of water each. She handed them out to Oscar, Julian, and Seb, each sat in chairs spread across the living room.

Despite the gesture, no one spoke.

Oscar knew the others could see he was seething. That he was furious – this was *their* suggestion. He had fought against the idea, he had told them it was not good, he had told them it–

No.

He'd been having the same argument with them in his mind ever since he got in the car.

But how could he say anything?

His mistake had potentially led to Hell on Earth. How could he point out how wrong they'd all been?

He wondered whether they were thinking the same, or whether they were deeming this as a necessary casualty. After all, wars always have casualties.

But surely, some casualties could be avoided.

He didn't touch his coffee. Didn't touch his water. He let the coffee sink to a mildly warm temperature, knowing April's eyes were on him but not returning her stare. She was waiting for him to take a sip, as if a sip would indicate he was coping, he was forgiving her – and, despite being thirsty and knowing it was spiteful, he intentionally didn't touch the drink.

Julian stood up and went to the toilet. The toilet eventually flushed and he returned, sitting on the exact same chair in the exact same position.

Finally, Julian was the one to speak.

"We need to decide on our next move," he stated.

Oh, Julian. Ever the straight talker.

Oscar scowled and tutted, burying his face beneath his hand.

"This might not be the best time," April said.

"We can't afford to pick a best time. People are potentially dying in that hospital–" Oscar lifted his head and looked at Julian, frowning at the poor choice of words. "–At least, more people are potentially dying. It's up to us to do something. We can't sit around and wait."

"I know, Julian, I know we can't. But you can at least give us all a minute."

"I've given you about an hour."

Oscar huffed. He really didn't want this argument. A confrontation with Julian's stubborn diatribe was not what he needed right now.

He stood and directed himself to the door.

"Where are you going?" Julian demanded, and Oscar stopped.

He slowly turned his head to Julian, his eyelids lowering, realising just how tired he was.

He didn't answer. Just looked to Julian in a way that showed exactly what he thought of him. The resentment, irritation, ill-timed rants. It was all too much. What was he even hoping to accomplish?

"It's our duty," Julian persisted. "We have to figure out a plan of attack. We have to go back."

"Maybe we shouldn't," April suggested, her voice quiet and timid, so unlike her. "If we need to think of this on a bigger scale, then we all need to be alive for the world to stand a chance. If we go back, and we're all dead, we're useless to anyone."

"Well, it's a risk, isn't it?"

"I'm not sure about taking any more risks, Julian."

Seb nudged the curtains to the side and looked out the window. His eyes widened, like he'd seen something. He looked back to Oscar, something in his face, something worried, on edge.

"What is it?" Oscar asked, but was spoken over.

"We need to be stronger than that," Julian continued. "We're going to fail many times, we're going to have lots of setbacks – we need to have the confidence and resolve to come back from them."

"But we also need to think clearly."

"Er, guys," Seb tried to interject, but his voice was lost amongst the conflict.

Oscar tried to listen to Seb, tried to find out what it was that was alarming him, what he was seeing outside.

"We need to be together on this," Julian claimed.

"Together? We haven't been together since you decided to hang onto your grudge."

"I have to be honest."

"No, you have to be nasty."

"Guys," Seb tried to interrupt again, failing. "Seriously."

"I am not being nasty. Surely you know me better than that."

"I'm not even sure anymore."

"Guys, really, listen," Seb tried again.

"Shut up," Oscar tried saying, straining to see what Seb wanted to say.

"I took you off the streets!"

"Yeah, over a decade ago – that isn't going to save you from every argument."

"Julian, April, shut up!" Oscar shouted. They both looked to him agape. He ignored them and directed his arm toward Seb, indicating it was okay for him to talk. "What is it?"

"Er, there's… there's people outside," Seb said.

"What, at the door?"

"No. As in, there are people standing outside. Lots of them. Standing outside the house. And they don't look right."

OSCAR KNOCKED THROUGH THE DOORWAYS OF EACH ROOM, peering through the curtains, squinting at the night.

They were everywhere.

Humans with nothing human about them.

A mass of deadened faces. Standing stationary around the house, outside every window, empty, gormless, yet full of rage.

Pale skin clung to the bones of their faces, scabs hanging from their cheeks, eyes flickering red. Their bodies stood limp, like they were hanging from invisible rope, and in their wrathful eyes Oscar could see the evil beneath the surface.

They didn't move. Didn't speak. Didn't break their empty grimace.

Oscar had seen enough victims of demonic possession to know what was wrong with them. His mind went back to Margaret Kummings and the strength that just she alone had displayed.

They could barely handle *one*.

He rushed back into the living room where everyone was stood. Julian pacing back and forth, Seb pressed up against the wall, April fidgeting with her hands.

"They are everywhere," Oscar said. "All around the house. Out the front, the garden, the side of the house. Everywhere."

"What do they want?" Seb asked, a tremble in his voice he couldn't hide.

"Isn't it obvious?" barked Julian. "So often we've gone to them, brought the fight to them. Now they are bringing the fight to us."

"Why?" Seb cried.

"Because they can. Because now they are strong enough to come to us, now they can outnumber us and out-strength us."

Oscar searched his pocket for his crucifix.

"But why now?" April mused.

"Why now?" Julian retorted. "Each one of them has a demon inside of them, and we are the only threat in their way, even if we are a very small threat."

Julian looked around the scared faces gazing back at him.

"They are looking to end it," he said, and left a moment for his statement to hang on the air like a potent odour. "They know what happened at the psychiatric unit. They know we're vulnerable; that we're defeatable. Now is the perfect time."

"So what do we do?" Seb asked.

The question lingered between them, unanswered.

"Could we fight them?" Oscar suggested, knowing it was a stupid proposal as soon as he said it.

They all looked at each other, knowing they needed to act fast, but no one knowing how to act.

They were outnumbered. Outpowered. Outdone.

There was no fighting them, and they knew it. Hell wouldn't send its minions without ultimate confidence that they would win.

Oscar tried to think how they had let this happen. How they had become so susceptible that they had thought to bring the fight to them.

The Sensitives had always been in control. Always been the

ones to show up, fight a demon, then go home like it was just another day at work.

This wasn't just another day at work.

This was the beginning of the end, and they knew it, though none of them would say it aloud.

"They are coming closer," Seb said, looking out between the crack in the curtains. "I think they have weapons."

"Get away from the window!" Julian demanded, and Seb hastily obeyed.

"Weapons?" Oscar said. He hadn't seen weapons, but it had been dark. "Sorry, but I have to see this."

He opened the crack in the curtains and closed it just as quickly.

Seb was right.

They were walking toward the house, synchronised, slow steps, their hands holding knives or hatchets or axes or blades or...

"We're screwed," Oscar muttered without intending to.

"We barricade ourselves in," Julian concluded. "We wait it out."

"Wait it out? How are we supposed to wait it out?" Oscar retorted.

"Got another idea?"

"We call the Vatican."

"And they do what? We're the ones that they would send to a situation like this." Julian looked across the scared faces. "We are on our own."

Those words pressed themselves into Oscar's mind like a handprint in sand.

We are on our own.

Oscar felt it like he'd never felt it before.

"Fine," he said. "Let's get the furniture up against the entrances."

Just as he said it, he heard the door handle of the front door buckle.

"Did we lock it?" April asked.

OSCAR BARGED AGAINST THE FRONT DOOR, SLAMMING IT CLOSED just as it began to open. He turned the lock, put the chain on, then stepped away.

The door handle continued to move, up and down, up and down. The door buckled under the strength of whatever was charging against it.

"The door's not going to hold," he said, feeling April at his side.

The door shook even harder. Violent rattles trembling its hinges.

Julian backed out of the living room, carrying one end of the sofa and Seb the other, and they pushed it against the door.

The sofa shook under the shudder of the door frame.

"It's not going to hold," Oscar said.

"I'll see what I can find," Seb said, rushing back into the living room.

"What about the rest of the house?" April said.

Oscar ran through the kitchen to the back door that led to the garden; a door made entirely of glass. Two contorted faces pressed against the glass, sharpened blades in their hands.

One of them was trying to open the door.

Oscar checked the lock was turned and rushed through the kitchen to the small utility room, where he found another demented face pressed up against the window of the side door. He turned the lock.

"We need to barricade these doors!" he shouted.

No one answered him. All he heard were the movements of more furniture and the slamming against the front door.

Every entrance to the house buckled. The front door, back door, utility room door – every one of them shook under the pull of vacant vessels with demonic strength.

They were going to get in.

Oscar knew it. He felt it.

He grabbed the kitchen table and turned it on its side, pushing it up against the back door. It covered the bottom half but did little to deter the attempts to break down the threshold, and Oscar looked up just in time to see a fist retract and launch into the glass.

The glass cracked.

The man retracted his fist again, slamming it into the glass, causing the crack to grow.

"Shit," Oscar exclaimed.

The utility room door shook.

He took two dining chairs and dragged them to the utility room, lodging one beneath the door handle and the other atop it against the glass.

The kitchen door cracked further.

He made his way back to the kitchen, just in time to see the entire window smash.

The first man stepped in, a curved blade at his side. Followed by a woman holding an axe. Followed by a pre-pubescent girl wielding a pair of grass trimmers.

Oscar looked around him.

Watching them progress toward him.
Watching them ready their weapons.
They were inside the house.

37

EVERYWHERE SEB LOOKED, HE FOUND FURNITURE TOO SMALL TO be effective, but he couldn't wait any longer. He couldn't. Whatever was there would just have to do.

He picked up the coffee table, dropping Oscar's still full coffee on the floor. A stain didn't particularly matter at this point.

He brought it through to Julian, who was pressing against the barricaded front door. The door seemed to have begun to crack, a thin line running past the handle.

"Yes, Seb!" came Oscar's voice.

Seb saw them in the kitchen, moving in on Oscar. Three of them – and behind that three, more walking in. He panicked, a sting of pain in his heart, most likely caused by the strain of bursting against his ribs.

Oscar ran inside and shut the kitchen door. He tried to hold it close, but struggled – it kept opening, and Oscar kept slamming it back again.

If that door opened, they were all dead.

"Seb, I need your help!" Oscar demanded.

Seb dropped the coffee table and ran to Oscar's side, pressing his shoulder against the door.

Damn, they were strong.

The door still opened against their resistance, but each time, they managed to shut it again.

They weren't going to be able to hold it closed forever.

"April!" Oscar shouted over his shoulder. "Find something we can barricade with!"

April rushed into the living room. Seb knew she wouldn't find much, but he didn't have time to say anything.

Putting all his weight against the door, straining his muscles, pushing with his shoulder, his arm, his hand, his thigh, pressing his feet against the floor for leverage – he looked to the side of him.

Oscar was still there, struggling with him, trying to hold the door closed. Knowing that they probably weren't going to make it.

Behind him, Julian pushing a sofa against a door that was beginning to crack open.

From his side, April trying to push an armchair through the living room, struggling to get it through the width of the doorframe.

"I can't get it through," she said, and tried turning it on its side, but struggled against its weight.

Watching them, experiencing the torment, witnessing the bloodshed – Seb felt sad. Resolved.

In an instant, he changed.

No more meaningless endeavours to bed every woman he met.

No more ill-timed jokes at the expense of the situation.

No more inability to take anything seriously, never committing, always searching for the anecdote.

He let it go.

If he managed to survive this, he would be different.

If he managed to survive.

If he was one of them, as they so definitively claimed, it was time to grow up.

April gave up trying to push the chair through. It wouldn't fit.

"I can't, Oscar. I can't."

The kitchen door opened again and an arm found its way through. It stuck there, between the doorframe and the door.

Oscar repeatedly punched the arm, but it did nothing. The arm did not deter. It crept out, more and more of it becoming visible.

"April, just come help us then!" Oscar instructed.

April walked forward but stopped, and fell to her knees

"April?" Oscar shouted.

She collapsed to her back. Her eyes widened, like she was in a trance, and her breath became stuck somewhere in her throat.

"April!"

Oscar went to leave the door but realised he couldn't. If they came in, they were all dead, including April.

But April was in trouble.

"April, talk to me!" he shouted.

Seb looked away from her. He couldn't take it. Not another death. Not her.

"April!" Oscar repeated.

The arm crept further in, a shoulder joining it. Oscar tried punching it, but the hand clamped around his wrist and grabbed hold, preventing him from pushing against the door, allowing the man to push his head through, followed by his body.

Then he barged the door open.

Then he entered.

Oscar fell to his back, then crawled over to April's side.

"April, please," he whimpered, though he knew it didn't matter. They were all about to die.

Seb punched the nearest face but it did nothing. They just looked back at him like he'd brushed his fingers against their broken skin.

The front door kicked open and the sofa was pushed aside, along with Julian.

Seb withdrew his crucifix, hoping it would save him.

It wouldn't.

38

APRIL HAD LEFT THE ROOM.

She felt the commotion in a far-off place, heard the fighting, the shouting, felt the fear – but she was not there. In body, yes, but not in mind.

In her mind she saw her. Running.

"Thea…" she spoke.

Thea lifted her head, as if she heard, as if April's tone was different to all the other voices attacking her.

"Thea, I see you, you're on the right path."

"Leave me alone!" Thea cried. "Tell them to leave me alone!"

"They will, Thea, they will, but you have to get to us first. Can you do that?"

"Yes! I want to! But I can't find you!"

"Just follow my voice, Thea, follow my voice."

April pushed her way into the girl's mind, felt the mixture of confusion and terror and agony and perplexity and – oh, poor girl. Poor, poor girl.

She was so hurt.

So distraught.

She had no idea about her power.

"That's it, Thea."

"Leave me alone!" Thea screamed, though April knew it wasn't at her.

"You're doing well, Thea, you're doing brilliantly, just keep going."

Thea collapsed to her knees.

She couldn't take any more.

In her mind, April could see, Thea wanted to end it. To end the shouts, the voices, the visions, the smells, the sounds – her head was full up with clutter, mess at every corner, and she was struggling to make herself out amongst the chaos.

"You're still in there, Thea. You're strong, you can do this."

Thea shook her head. Wept. Bowed her head to the floor, buried it in the muddy soil. It was raining hard now, coming in all directions from the hits of the leaves and branches above her.

But she was so close.

So, so close.

"Thea, you have to trust me."

"No!"

Thea searched for something. Something to end it, something to stop the constant fighting. Inside her mind was like a messy room where everything was there but you just couldn't find anything, everything was buried under something else, everything out of place – in a state that you look at and think, *how the hell am I going to tidy this?*

But April knew she could help Thea tidy it; she knew she could.

"Please, Thea…"

Thea shook her head.

"Keep going…"

She felt her connection loosen. She had to keep it.

She wasn't breathing. April felt her body weaken. Thea was

sucking her life from her and April couldn't hang on much longer for fear of losing her own life.

"Thea, come on," April pleaded.

"No…"

"Thea, I–"

"*Enough!*"

Her scream shattered April's mind, the shoot of a migraine hitting all corners of her skull.

Her eyes abruptly opened and she was back in the house, gasping for air, suffocating on oxygen.

Oscar was sat over her, saying her name, pleading with her.

Behind Oscar, there they were. Inside.

All of them coming forward.

Raising their weapons.

Ready to strike.

39

THE RAIN MIXED WITH THE WHISPERS, CREATING A SYMPHONY OF noise, a constant assault on Thea's mind. She buried her head in her hands, not caring about getting mud on her face or her elbows or her knees.

Who cares about mud if you're just about to die?

Suicide seemed like the only answer.

But that woman...April...she said she could help her...

Kill yourself.

Do it.

End it.

It's all too much.

You're not worth it.

Just die.

The dead seemed to agree.

Were they all the dead? Or were they something else?

Demons, maybe. She heard someone mention it once. She'd seen it on television. She assumed these were people passed on, but she could be wrong.

She was always wrong.

About everything. Always.

She missed her brother.

Death could either be the end or a chance to be reunited.

It would be hard on her parents. Two children, both of them ending their lives.

For all they knew, she could be lying in a ditch, dead, bleeding – they had no idea where she was. She'd been missing for at least a day now. Maybe there was a police search for her. She wondered what they would be saying. *Mentally ill girl missing, brother just died, huge risk.*

Was she a huge risk? Did they see her that way?

She already knew she was a burden.

She was always a burden. To everyone she knew.

Would she be a burden to April?

If they knew what she could do, if they could help...

She lifted her head and screamed, roared out her thoughts, roared out her anguish, roared out her despair. She'd had enough of thinking, enough of hearing, she wanted it all to just stop.

The sweet release of sleep never gave her a break. She couldn't sleep when she was surrounded by a dozen voices with a dozen taunts and a dozen sick requests.

And the voices had been getting sicker.

I sodomise your brother in Hell...

I touched your filthy cunt...

I'll fill your body with your father...

She wiped the rain out of her hands.

Looked up.

Was there a God? Was he listening? Did he know?

Or was this in her head?

If there was evil, there must be good.

But why were they speaking to her?

How could she end it?

A river, nearby, maybe. Drowning. Sinking under, suffocating on mouthfuls of water.

She slumped on her back and lay in the dirt, facing up at the rain. It pelted her face but she didn't care. It stung, but a good stinging. One that she relished, one that let her know the rain was real.

The bushes shuffled and the shadows chased. Bodies walked by her head, faces down, contorted visages in smoke flew over her.

She didn't react.

She'd seen it all before.

She closed her eyes. Wondered if she just lay there, would she die.

Like her brother.

Die like her brother.

Do to her parents what her brother did.

Her eyes opened.

She couldn't. She owed it to him to give it one more try. To get to April, to see what she could do. Were there more of them, or was it just her?

She pushed herself to her knees, then to her feet. She marched onwards.

Somehow, she knew where she was going. She felt the voice before her.

She decided to run. To sprint.

She made it out of the wooded area and to an estate. A cluster of houses fixed together around entwining roads.

This was where she was.

She ran through the paths, over the gravel, across the lawn.

She saw them from far off.

Bodies. Standing. Weapons. Surrounding a house.

That was the house.

It was under attack.

Could she help them?

Their faces turned toward her. Glared at her.

She felt something surge within her, like anger but more

glorious. She lifted her hands into the air. She saw the tremble of their faces.

She opened her mouth and screamed. The scream carried a roar across the rain with a ferocity she couldn't have precedented. The faces staring at her backed away, their bodies stepped away.

They fled.

In every direction, like flies scampering away from a footstep.

They were gone within seconds.

The door to the house had been smashed open.

She entered.

On the floor, she saw April. Next to her was a man. By the door, against a sofa that had been barricaded against the entrance, another man. Across the room, another man.

And more of *them*. Stood over these people. Weapons in their hands, faces of evil, eyes of hate – staring at them like they were about to kill them.

They will not kill them.

She wouldn't let them.

She clenched her fists and roared once more, shutting her eyes tight and opening again just to see them fleeing out of the far, smashed kitchen door.

They all stood. The ones who were being attacked, and now were saved.

They all stood and looked to Thea.

"Thea…" April said, approaching her.

Faces of recognition adorned the rest.

Somehow, she knew them. Although she'd never met them, she knew them. They were like her. She was one of them.

She fell to her knees.

She hadn't realised how weak she was.

Whatever she'd done, it had taken everything she had.

"Help… me…"

April rushed to her side, putting a hand on her back, a hand on her cheek, brushing her sweaty, rain-drenched hair out of her face, her face covered in rain and mud.

"It's okay," April reassured her.

April's voice was far away.

The room was hazy.

She collapsed in April's arms, and finally got that sleep she was so desperately after.

THEN

SAT IN YE OLDE BLACK BEAR, IN THE CORNER FARTHEST FROM other life, Julian held his hand loosely around the base of his pint. It was an old pub, an exterior of bumpy white with black panels in wonky lines, and an interior full of low-hanging ceilings and wooden beams. It was quiet now, and he was able to sit in the corner away from the jobless and the students nursing their pints, but it wasn't always so quiet. He had grown up with this pub. He'd been there on a Friday night and he'd seen the wreckage the drunks did to the ageing building come closing time.

It was one of those pubs that boasted the label of *Most Haunted Pub in the United Kingdom* – a label that pretty much any pub over two hundred years old seemed to boast. As far as Julian was concerned, the people who claimed such labels weren't aware of the reality behind it. To them a gimmick they could use to lure the odd ghost hunter, someone idiotic who had no idea what evil they were trying to confront.

He gulped down a few more mouthfuls of lager and slammed the pint glass back on the coaster to find a third of it gone.

He belched and didn't care about the over-shoulder glance from the bearded man at the bar. The man that was in there every day on his own – like Julian cared for the judgement of such a bum. Julian did something meaningful with his life; this guy drank beer from 9.30 a.m. Fuck him. He can go to Hell.

They can all go to Hell.

He gulped down another third and regretfully stared at the last swig left in the glass.

That afternoon replayed in his mind for what was probably the hundredth time.

Guilty.

They'd found him guilty.

Derek Lansdale, legendary supernatural expert, lecturer in paranormal studies, PhD, mentor, friend, support, role model – behind bars, hidden away like he was scum.

Those people knew nothing of the man they had sent down.

And for neglect

Fucking neglect.

Jesus.

If Derek hadn't acted in the way he had, attempted to perform the exorcism with the energy he showed, then that would be *neglect.*

As it was, he did everything for that girl and now he was being punished for it.

And the girl was dead.

He bowed his head and wished he didn't have to get up to buy his fifth beer and that it would just appear before him.

Derek had been clear about what Julian's actions were to be.

Julian was to recruit Sensitives. He was to find those like him, and he was to use them to address the balance, to fight demons and ensure that Hell kept quiet for as long as he was physically able.

He was meant to surround himself with people like him.

People like him.

So, if that was what he was meant to do – then why did he feel so alone?

He threw back the final sips of his pint and staggered to the bar.

"Another," he grunted at the barmaid. He realised this was a different barmaid than had served him last, but she saw his drink of choice from the brand on his empty pint glass and went about pouring his drink.

He looked at the man with a beard who was always there from early morning to late night, sitting at the bar.

The man looked back.

Julian didn't look away. The piece of shit could break first. What was the point?

Suddenly, he felt drunk.

"What did you do?" Julian asked.

"Excuse me?" the man replied.

"What did you do? I mean, to get to where you are now. What did you do?"

"I don't know what you're talking about, son."

Julian waved a hand at the man as if to dismiss him. It slowly occurred to him that *this could be me someday*. He willed the thought away and collected his full pint glass, handing a scrunched-up five-pound note to the barmaid.

"Can you get some more of the house red from downstairs for us?" a manager requested of the barmaid.

"From the cellar?" the barmaid said. "You're having a laugh!"

"Well, I'm not going down there."

"And neither am I."

The man huffed and walked on. Julian turned to the barmaid, intrigued.

"Why won't you go down there?" he asked, trying not to slur his words and trying not to let his eyelids droop in the way they did when he was starting to get drunk.

"None of us will. There's wine that's been down there for

years, none of us will get it."

"Why?" Julian repeated – evidently, she hadn't heard what his question was the first time.

"Because there's something down there."

"What?"

"They say it's a Lancastrian soldier."

Julian blurted out a loud, "Hah!"

"Laugh all you want, it's true," she said, then moved to the other side of the bar to serve another customer.

Bollocks. Absolute bollocks. Julian knew it, the barmaid probably knew it; Hell even the loser on the bar stool probably knew it.

Tewkesbury was famous for being part of the War of the Roses – one of many English civil wars for the throne in the 1400s. The towns-people here loved it, tourists loved it – there was even a medieval fayre every year where the locals dressed up like Tudor people and bashed their drums and basically gave Julian a thumping headache.

Of course, being the place of a bloody battle led to stories of soldiers who still hadn't moved on, who had come to a horrible end. Julian knew that if such spirits had lingered, they would be long gone by now. Almost six-hundred years later, they would have moved on or dissipated.

If something was in that cellar – which he highly doubted – then it would not be the spirit of a soldier.

Taking a swig of his pint, he glanced over at the barmaid, who had her back to him. Looking for onlookers, he snuck past the nearest beam, behind the bar, and to the steps that led to the cellar.

They were steep, stone steps. Julian had to take each one sideways in order to fit the length of his foot. Once he reached the bottom step, he withdrew his phone and shone its light into the darkness.

A soft, damp floor made his shoes wet. He made gentle

splashes as he meandered through, using the stone wall to guide him. Boxes of unopened wine sat in the far corner.

What a waste.

"All right then," Julian said. "Mr Lancastrian soldier, if that's what you are, which you are definitely not..."

He stumbled, tried not to spill his pint.

"...Then show yourself. I'm a Sensitive. I can take it."

He waited.

Nothing.

Just as he expected.

"Bunch of fucking idiots," he grunted.

A growl clung to the air.

He grinned. Did he really hear that?

"Okay then, Billy Big Balls, where are you?"

Nothing.

He shook his head.

"Bloody ghost my arse."

Just as he said it, something flew at him, a face on the smoke, with a roar that pushed him onto his back.

His pint glass shattered against the wall as it flung out of his hand.

"Shit!" he gasped.

He wanted to fight it. He did.

But without Derek, he didn't know what to do.

Alone, he didn't know what to do.

Maybe he'd come back here someday when he wasn't alone.

But for now, his arms were shaking, his bones were wobbling, and he was struggling to get himself back to his feet.

He scampered up the steps, using both his hands and his toes, and dove onto the floor.

With a confused glance from the barmaid, he sprinted for the exit and fled.

He never did return, and whatever was in the cellar remained as undisturbed as the wine.

NOW

A CIGARETTE NESTLED BETWEEN SEB'S FINGERS LIKE A FAVOURITE pen. Sat on the edge of the porch, he took a long drag, closing his eyes and relishing its warmth.

He patted the end of the cigarette, dropping the ash onto the grass. Noticing a few more shards of glass, he shifted further along the porch.

Behind him, Julian appeared in the doorframe. Julian walked carefully through the glass and took a seat next to Seb.

Morning was arriving, but none of them had had any sleep. It was a shame, because he was tired, and it was a beautiful sunrise – one he wished he could enjoy more.

"I didn't know you smoked," Julian observed.

"I don't," Seb answered, stubbing out the cigarette. "I just used to, and I found some in the bottom of my bag. Figured, what the hell."

"Yeah, I figure that a lot."

Seb looked at Julian, whose face appeared torn between thoughts. He looked reflective, as if he was thinking back on the night and wondering where it all went wrong.

"It was great that the girl – what's her name?" Seb asked.

"Thea."

"Yeah – it was great that Thea came along. Whatever she did, it seemed to work. She saved us."

"Nah, we were lucky."

Seb wondered if Julian just disagreed with everything everyone said, or whether he really did feel that way.

"Lucky?" Seb refuted. "Something brought Thea. *April* – brought Thea."

"Well, then, good for April. If Thea turns out to be who we think she is, then…"

Seb watched Julian some more. Julian's expression was a constant fight between vacancy and frowning.

"Do you ever look on the positive side, or what?" Seb asked.

"The positive side of what?"

"I don't know. Life. What happened. We were lucky, but, you know, thank God we were lucky!"

"God has little to do with it. He never bothers to lend a hand."

"It's an expression."

"Yeah, I know."

Julian huffed.

"So what about you?" he asked.

"What about me?"

"What are your thoughts? We were almost, very nearly killed."

"I think I can see things better now," Seb replied honestly. "I think I…I dunno."

"I know what you mean."

"What?"

"I felt it too, when I was your age. And I saw things for real. And I realised I needed to grow up and stop being mad at the world."

Seb laughed. "And when are you going to stop being mad at the world?"

At first, Julian scowled at the remark, then couldn't help but chuckle.

"I'm less mad than I was."

"You've got two good friends, at least. Oscar and April seem to have your back."

Julian's face dropped. Any sign of playfulness, of chuckling, joking, positivity, all left. Replaced by the resuming look of despondency.

Without another word, Julian stood and walked back inside.

Ah, well. Seb was starting to get used to it. Maybe the guy was just moody; who cares?

He looked out to the sunrise and thought about what really mattered. About the great universe before him, the greater purpose at his feet, the way he could help.

"Hey, Seb," Oscar said from behind him.

Seb turned around to see Oscar stood with a hammer and some new panes of glass.

"Mind giving me a hand?"

Seb laughed. This wasn't what he meant when he said he wanted to help, but it would do.

"What is it?" Oscar asked.

"Nothing," Seb answered. "Nothing at all."

THE SOFT, DELICATE SCENT OF FRESH BEDSHEETS ACCOMPANIED the glorious ray of sun through the window. As Thea opened her eyes, she lifted her hand to shield them, wondering why the curtains weren't fully closed.

Had her parents opened them in the night? Her mum often sleepwalked and did strange things, such as open the fridge door and stare, or readjust furniture.

But, as she looked around herself, she realised she wasn't in her own bedroom. The sound of her parents making breakfast downstairs did not exist, and the smell of burnt toast did not find her.

She was alert.

Had she been kidnapped?

What had happened?

But, if she was kidnapped, why would they settle her into a comfortable bed in a decluttered bedroom with a vase of flowers on the bedside table?

Her clothes were on the radiator beneath the window, drying off.

Why were they drying off? She remembered being wet… wet and confused…but how? Why?

She looked down. She was wearing a set of pyjamas she didn't know. The trousers were a pattern of various shades of blue, and the t-shirt was white with a picture of an avocado over her heart.

She tried to remember. Closed her eyes and racked her brain.

She had been in the woods. Running. Wet.

Hearing things all the time.

She had come to this house.

Why wasn't she hearing anything now? Why had all the voices stopped? Where were the faces?

What was going on?

A gentle knock on the door announced itself and the door cracked open. A face poked in – male, scruffy, mid-to late-twenties.

"You're awake," the man observed. "Mind if I come in?"

If he was her captor, he was very polite.

She gave a feeble nod.

He walked in and gently closed the door behind him, being sensitive to the pounding in her head.

She hadn't even realised she had such a bad headache. She massaged her temples, hoping it would help.

"Those are April's pyjamas, by the way," the man said. "In case you were wondering. She changed you, not any of the rest of us."

He placed a glass of water and some paracetamol on the bedside table. She was immediately grateful, popping out two pills followed by a few mouthfuls of water.

"Who's April? Where am I?"

"Oh, I am sorry, I should probably explain. Mind if I sit?"

He took a chair from the corner of the room. Once she had

shaken her head to say she didn't mind, he placed it next to her bed, but not too close, and sat casually.

"My name is Oscar. April is my girlfriend. Julian is also one of us, as is Seb, who is an apprentice, someone who's learning, like you. And…well, we did have someone else, but…not anymore. Now we have you – Thea. Don't be worried that we know your name. April can see things like that."

"I don't understand."

"You're a Sensitive. Like us."

Oscar proceeded to give her the spiel. Told her what a Sensitive was, what they did, the history of how they came together. He recounted what had happened the previous night, and how she had come to help. Then, hoping not to overwhelm her but knowing she needed the truth, he began to elaborate on their grave predicament. About what was at stake and about the limited time and resources they had to deal with it.

"Wow…" she said, widening her eyes to keep herself awake. Despite having just woken up, she was still so tired.

"Which brings us to you. I assume you've been hearing things."

"Yes…" Thea confirmed, her intrigue piquing. "Yes, I have."

"You don't need to worry; you're not crazy. I assume you don't hear them now?"

"No."

"That's because such things rarely come to where a group of Sensitives live. At least, not until last night. Your mind should be more peaceful here."

She ran her hands over her face and through her hair. She could feel dried sweat clinging to her skin and she craved a shower.

"We can help you, Thea. We *will* help you. We all have gifts like you, but we can all control it."

"Is there something wrong with me?"

"Actually, Thea, you may just be the very thing this world

needs." He leant forward. "In this war, we have been missing something. A Sensitive with a gift far stronger than the rest of us, with far more of Heaven in them than any other. This person could decide everything."

"And, this person, you think it might be...me?"

Oscar leant back in his chair, suddenly conscious that he may be coming on a little strong.

"Maybe," he said. "I don't want to put too much on your shoulders too soon. I know you've been struggling, I know things have been hard. I just...we don't have much time. So if I'm overwhelming you, I'm sorry, but I don't have much choice."

She stared back at him blankly.

"Listen, why don't I leave you to it. Let you clean up, digest everything, have a bit of space. Come downstairs when you're ready, and I'll introduce you to everyone. That sound all right?"

She nodded, delicately, staring vacantly at the floor.

Oscar stood and put the chair back.

"Maybe you should phone your parents, too. I imagine they'd be worried."

Oh, God, my parents...

They must be terrified. Despairing. They just lost their son, now they didn't know where their daughter was.

Then again, she didn't know where she was.

Or who she was.

THE HEAVY STREAM OF WATER FROM THE SHOWERHEAD FELT refreshing as it cascaded over Thea's body.

She stood with her hand against the wall, her head down, the water dripping down the back of her head, letting the power of the spray cleanse away the last few weeks. It was nice to have burning water cleaning her rather than rainwater muddying her.

Water dribbled down her forehead in streams, meeting at her bottom lip, then dribbling the vertical drop to her toes. The water running down her wasn't clear, wasn't clean – it was filthy. Slabs of mud and greenish liquid washed off her prickly legs. The attachment of sweat and rain and anguish departed, disappearing down the drain with a hefty gurgle.

Her fingers wrinkled, and she decided it was enough. She turned the shower off and felt instantly cold. She wrapped a towel around her – it was a big, comforting towel, the kind her grandparents used to have when she visited them as a child – then used another to dry her hair. Her arms grew weary quickly, and she gave up with her hair still damp – it would have to do.

As she stepped lightly across the landing, she could hear voices below, talking, the rest of these Sensitives. The people who were apparently like her.

For all she knew, they were crazy. They were deranged, strange weirdos who wanted to make her part of their illusion.

But, if they were crazy, so was she.

And she had a very strong feeling she wasn't.

Just as she had a very strong feeling that she should trust these people. That these people had the answers, that they would guide her.

She found their cordless landline phone perched on a table in the bedroom at the far side of the corridor. She took it and crept back into her room, unsure why she was creeping, and shut the door.

Someone had laid out clothes for her. She assumed it was April – the person she'd seen in her mind, the person that had spoken to her. Either way, she was grateful for the clean clothes, and it seemed like April had quite a cool fashion sense. Once she'd put on the jeans and black t-shirt that read *Guns n' Roses* across it, she picked up the phone and stared at it.

She knew the number.

She knew she should.

But it had never been so hard.

Closing her eyes, breathing, listening to the silence, the first silence she'd heard in a long time, she tried to talk herself out of it.

Did she really need to speak to them?

Would it make any difference?

No, she had to. Especially after everything, they would be too worried.

Forcing her fingers to move, she dialled in her parents' number and put the phone to her ear. It only rang twice before it was answered.

"Hello?" came the tired voice of her mum.

"Hi, Mum."

A sudden commotion came from the other end of the phone, her mother weeping, stifling tears. It was in that moment Thea realised just what she'd put her parents through.

"Oh, Thea! Thea! Thank God you're okay! Oh my God, we've been so worried, we've been so, so worried!"

"It's okay, Mum. It's okay. I'm okay."

"Oh, God, Thea, I thought you were dead, I thought they were going to find you in a ditch somewhere, the police have been out, the neighbourhood has been searching the nearby area for you! Oh, Thea, thank God you are okay!"

"I am, honestly, Mum. You can tell everyone to go home. I'm fine."

"Where are you?"

Thea hesitated. She knew the question was going to come, she just hadn't thought about how to answer it.

"I'm at a friend's house," she answered.

"Which friend? I'll come pick you up."

"No, Mum. I don't need to be picked up."

In the silence that followed Thea was sure she could hear her mum's world crashing around her.

"What?"

"I – I just need a few day's space, just to clear my head. Make sure everything is okay."

"But, Thea…"

"No, Mum. I'm safe, I'm fine, I wanted to let you know that. You can take me off as a missing person, tell everyone I'm okay. I've not been abducted, I'm not being held against my will. It's just…just…this is something I have to do."

Her mum said nothing.

"Sorry."

"Okay, Thea. Okay. Just – just let us know you're safe, every day, okay?"

"I will."

"And when you're ready to come home, know that we're here. We love you and we're here, and we miss you so, so much."

"I miss you too, Mum."

"Oh, Thea, we love you, we love you so much."

"I'm going to go now... Bye, Mum."

"Goodbye, Thea."

She hung up.

She stood still, holding the receiver, letting the conversation sink over her.

She walked statically back into the room, put the phone back, and made her way to the stairs. With little emotion, little movement, she walked robotically down the stairs and into the hallway.

From the kitchen, three men and a woman froze their conversation and stared at her.

The woman – April, she assumed – walked toward Thea. Slowly, as if approaching a dangerous animal.

Thea felt tears accrue in the corner of her eyes. Before she knew what was happening, she was on her knees, bawling, April's arms wrapped tightly around her. She sank into April's embrace, let April stroke her hair.

Everything came out.

In that single minute of non-stop crying, it all surfaced.

Her brother.

Her parents.

The voices.

The faces.

The threats.

School.

Mum.

Running through the forest with no idea where to go.

Fatigue, mental exhaustion, despair.

Everything poured out of her into April's arms. She felt bad for dampening April's sleeve, but April didn't seem to care. She was just there, like Thea needed someone there, to hold her tight, to keep her close.

And to tell her, just as April did, ever so softly – "Everything will be okay."

Thea believed her.

Finally, as Thea's tears died down, April cupped her face and forced her to look into April's eyes.

"We are so glad you're here, Thea," April told her. "So, so glad. You've done so well. You are so brave, Thea, so, so brave."

Thea didn't feel it, but she nodded nonetheless, appreciating the kind words April was showering over her.

In that moment, she realised she was in the right place. She was grateful she hadn't ended things. She was grateful she had come.

"Why don't we get you a hot drink and introduce you to people, yeah?"

Within minutes, Thea was sat at the kitchen table with a coffee, engrossed in conversation with those around her. Oscar spoke about how grateful he was for her arrival, just as he'd already done. Seb spoke about how much he'd learnt since he'd been here. Julian, who seemed a bit standoffish, smiled at her and told her that he, too, was pleased that she was here.

After an hour or so, the conversation died down and things became serious.

"Okay, Thea," Julian said. "I wouldn't normally rush you into this, but we don't have much time. Do you feel up to it?"

"Feel up to what?"

"Seeing what you can do. We know how good we think you are, now it's just time to prove it."

Thea looked to April, who nodded confirmation it was okay.

"Yes," she answered.

44

IT WAS SILLY, REALLY, BUT JULIAN STILL FELT A PANG OF FEAR AT the sight of Ye Olde Black Bear. The evil he'd confronted whilst moderately drunk in the wine cellar was little compared to what he'd faced since, but being there still conjured feelings of being a novice. The familiar walls and familiar smells and familiar creaks of floor made him feel like he was right back there again, begrudging Derek's guilty sentence, completely alone.

Then again, was he really any less alone now?

He led the group to the bar, where Seb ordered a round of drinks to distract the barman. Julian half expected to see the older man with a beard sat at the bar, but he didn't. He wondered if the man was still alive, or whether his alcohol addiction or loneliness had since taken his life.

With Seb ordering drinks, this allowed Oscar, Julian, and April to escort Thea into the cellar, cautiously stepping down, putting their hands on the cold, bumpy wall to balance themselves.

Why's it always a cellar or basement?

Julian snorted at his silly question, then avoided the odd look April gave him as a result.

The whole drive here he'd focussed on the road whilst Oscar and April coached Thea through dealing with the things she heard and the things she saw. Constantly reminding her to focus on something in front of her, something that was closer to her, therefore putting everything else far enough away that it was background noise.

She found it more difficult to quiet her surroundings than Oscar or April had – but then again, she wasn't like Oscar or April, was she?

She was more powerful, or so they were to believe.

By the light of their phones, Thea stood in the middle of the cellar, standing turgidly with her hands rooted to her side.

"Do you remember last night?" Oscar asked. "Do you remember when you screamed, when you defeated everyone in that one release of energy?"

"Vaguely…" Thea's small voice answered.

"That's what you need to do now, but more controlled. Once whatever's here shows itself, lift your hand out, and release that burst – but rein it in."

"Rein it in?"

"Yes. What you're releasing is paranormal energy – it's far more than any of ours, which is why we couldn't do what you did. But you have enough that you should be able to send it out in waves."

"I…I don't…"

April placed a hand on Thea's shoulder. "Relax. All Oscar is saying is that if you release as much as you did yesterday, then you could cause more damage than you want. You want to curtail it."

"Curtail it," Thea echoed in confirmation. From what Julian could perceive, he highly doubted she'd taken any of it in.

"Now," said Oscar. "Try and make contact. It's up to you."

Thea gave a timid nod, then closed her eyes and dropped her chin to her chest. She loosened her arms, stood still, carefully, motionless.

Julian watched her, as did Oscar and April, waiting. If this girl knew half of the hopes they had pinned on her, then the pressure would likely destroy her.

They could do without another loss.

The thought provoked buried feelings. They'd had to move on quickly since Maddie's death, finding no time to wait in war – but he felt they needed to confront it at some point, to deal with it. Oscar would be feeling that he was right and he needed that acknowledged, and Julian would need to quell those wishes somehow.

Thea lifted her hand, her palm open, stretched out before her.

A rustle came from across the room, and they each quickly turned their light toward it. Smoke was rising, forming, creating something from the shadows.

Thea's fingers pointed, tightened, strengthened. Her face curled up, as if she was gripping something that wasn't there, tightening her unseeable hold.

The smoke continued to twist and writhe and wriggle until a vague face presented itself, its vagueness lessening and giving way to solid features, definite lines to the outline of an inhuman expression.

April and Oscar exchanged glances.

Julian looked at them, but he wasn't involved in their glances – the two of them in their own little world again.

Thea's arm shook. A few crumbles of plaster collapsed from the wall. The smoky face grew stronger, into a sneer, into a growl, and flew forward.

In a sudden scream, Thea threw her raised arm forward, punching something they couldn't see.

The face floated upwards, dissolving, until it was gone.

Thea opened her eyes.

And it was done that quickly.

Astonishing.

Oscar and April rushed to her side, full of words like "Oh my God!" and "You did it!"

Even Julian felt a little excited, as well as a little relieved. This brought their chances from two percent to ten percent, as far as he was concerned. A great boost; but the war wasn't won yet.

"Well done," Julian said. "But let's not celebrate too much yet. There's still a long way to go."

The sense of celebration died down, smiles fading from the others. Oscar put his hand on Thea's back, ignoring what Julian had said.

"You did well, Thea. Really well."

With a glance at Julian that showed exactly what Oscar thought, he made his way up the stairs.

April and Thea followed, neither of them making eye contact with Julian.

He was last to walk up the stairs. And, when they reached the top, he wasn't included in the excited recalling of the story to Seb. Instead, he was left to sip his drink quietly, unwanted and unnoticed.

It had been his job to recruit these people.

He'd done that job.

Maybe that just meant his part was over.

45

Elijah had heard murmurs before he'd heard anything definite. Voices of people passing, echoes of conversations, frantic exchanges of frightened faces.

It wasn't until he stopped one of his colleagues and demanded to know what was happening that the unsettling truth was finally delivered to him.

"We are evacuating," the doctor told him. "We are going to lock the doors and leave."

"What?" Elijah said, louder than he'd intended. "And leave everyone in here?"

"It's not an ideal situation."

"These people rely on our care!"

The doctor looked back and forth, checking for prying ears.

"This is between us, okay?" the doctor said in a hushed voice.

"Fine."

"There have been three deaths in the past hour alone."

"Of patients?"

"Nurses. Patients who have been tied down and sedated,

somehow ripping out of their restraints and mauling the nurses to death."

"My God…"

"The authorities have instructed us to evacuate, and any further action they take will be up to them." A scream echoed down the corridor. "Excuse me."

The doctor ran reluctantly toward the screams, his final words repeating around Elijah's thoughts.

Any further action they take will be up to them.

What did that mean?

Any further action?

What, were they sending in riot police? The army?

Were they just going to barricade this place shut and leave everyone to themselves?

People were dying. He knew it. People were doing inhuman things, and all attempt at control had failed. Elijah hated that he understood, but in desperate situations, people did desperate things.

He made his way to the lift and pressed the button for the third floor. He'd stop at his locker, then he'd get the heck out of there – his phone was still in there, along with pictures and a watch his mother had given him on his twenty-first birthday.

The lift doors opened.

It was oddly quiet.

Having become so used to the screams and screeches, it became desperately unsettling that they were no longer there.

Deciding just to keep his wits about him, he made his way around the corner and toward the locker room.

Overhead, the lights began to flicker. Every one of them, simultaneously battering on and off.

He entered the locker room, finding himself eerily alone. He shoved everything he needed from his locker into his bag.

A drip from the shower startled him.

He looked over his shoulder. There was no one there. Just the small drop of liquid rhythmically dropping from the showerhead.

Get a grip...

He packed his bag quicker.

Once he'd finished, he left the locker room.

He stopped.

Didn't move.

Down the corridor, there was something...

A person...

An old lady. This shouldn't worry him so much, but in the past week he'd seen old ladies do ridiculous things.

She was hunched over, her back to him, shaking, muttering something.

She was in the direction he needed to go.

He looked over his shoulder, checking behind him, always feeling like he was being watched.

They were alone.

The only way out was past her.

He edged forward, keeping a hand out, never diverting his stare.

He went to speak, but wondered what he would say.

As he came closer, the words became clearer. Well, the sounds became clearer; the words still didn't make sense.

"Et e alioquin interficiemus te... Et e alioquin interficiemus te..."

Was it Latin?

It sounded like it.

Why was it always Latin? Why did they keep speaking Latin?

Damn it, he should have just left when those paranormal freaks fled the basement. That should have told him it was time to leave then and there.

"Ma'am?" he said softly.

She fell to an abrupt silence, her body stiffening, her head rising but never turning over her shoulder.

"Dicere audes, quam mihi…"

"I don't understand you, I – are you okay?"

"Ego sum iens ut quisque occidere…"

"Do you speak English?"

"Pars sordes tibi…"

He edged ever closer, so close, his hand out, ready…

He could see the lift a few yards past her.

"Elijah," came the voice of another nurse. Jessica, younger, new, someone who'd been shadowing him.

He looked to his side and her face appeared from a room next to him.

"Elijah, I'm glad I found you, I need your help with–"

Before he could shush her, before he could tell her to look or stop or not to talk or anything of the kind, the old lady had turned and pounced on her with the speed of nothing Elijah had seen before.

He flattened himself against the wall, staring with disbelief as this lady tore out Jessica's throat with her teeth, then turned and grinned at him with part of Jessica's oesophagus hanging between her canines.

He considered helping Jessica, but the lady dug her teeth into the poor woman's throat with everything it had and ripped out so much there was no way she could survive.

The sight of skin and blood and muscle dripping down the woman's chin was one that would never leave him.

He ran, ran with all he had, ran to the lift at the end of the corridor.

He heard her chasing, heard her rebounding off the walls, saw in the mirror of the lift as she carried herself on all fours like an animal on the hunt.

The lift doors shut just in time.

He went into his bag and withdrew his phone.

Just as his quivering hands fumbled his phone to an unlocked state, the lift doors opened, and Elijah met the chaos that was the bottom floor.

46

THE DOOR WAS SHUT, AND OSCAR WAS ALONE WITH JULIAN AND April again.

Thea had asked to be left to rest, and it was a fair request. After scanning their bookshelf for a book she would likely be too tired to read, she took a cup of tea upstairs and shut the bedroom door.

Seb had made himself comfortable in the living room, watching something on television.

Which meant they were left alone again.

The original three.

Oscar chuckled.

The original three.

It was more like April and Julian were the original two.

They had worked together for so long. Julian and Oscar had always, for some reason, had friction, but over the years, they had come to rely on each other and trust in each other's abilities. April had been close to both of them in different capacities. Yet now, it felt like they were far from being what they were just a few months ago.

Back when they still had a child.

Or, at least, back when they thought they did.

None of them sat. They all leant against the wall or the kitchen side at various points around the room, in deep contemplation.

"Well," Oscar said, attempting to voice a thought or a musing, but finding himself unable to verbalise the many perplexities of their past few days.

"I know," April said.

"I don't feel like we've even had a chance to adjust to what happened. I mean, with..."

Maddie.

He couldn't say her name aloud, so he thought it instead.

"It's..." April struggled to find the words. "I feel so guilty."

Oscar looked to Julian, waiting for him to say something similar. Confess feelings of guilt, of responsibility, acknowledgement that he contributed to the actions that led to her death.

"She chose to do it," Julian eventually said, feeling Oscar's stare. "We sanctioned it, yes, but ultimately, Maddie made the decision."

"Are you kidding?"

"We all have to take responsibility for–"

"She was a child. Under our guidance. How could–"

"Guys!" April snapped.

Oscar and Julian quelled their argument. Finding that they had both stood, they simmered back to their leaning positions.

"What has happened since is nothing short of a miracle," April said. "We need to be careful. We need to harness Thea, protect her, and guide her to becoming what she can be. She alone is our greatest weapon, and probably our only chance."

"Wrong," Julian stated.

"What?"

"I mean, you're right in that she is our greatest chance. But wrong in that we need to protect her. We need to put her on the front line and make some larger strides forward."

"Have you not learnt anything about taking risks?" Oscar asked.

"Like I said before, we have to take risks, and some of them won't come off – but if we don't take any, we don't stand a chance."

Oscar shook his head. He couldn't believe what he was hearing. When had Julian's decision-making become so…irrational? So misguided, determined to get them all killed?

"I know what I'm doing, Oscar," Julian stated.

"Well, you don't seem–"

"Derek left me in charge!" Julian shouted, so loud the new pane of glass in the door shook.

Julian had never shouted like this before.

In fact, in all Julian's nasty exchanges, Oscar was sure he'd never actually heard Julian shout at all.

"Or are you forgetting that?" Julian continued, standing and staring down Oscar and April. "I recruited you" – he jabbed a finger at April – "and, God help me, I recruited you" – he jabbed another finger at Oscar. "I was doing this long before either of you realised you could."

He gave a beat for objections to be voiced, but his outburst had silenced them.

"You remember Derek? Huh?" Julian spat. "You remember him? The guy who dedicated his life to this, the guy who fought a war against the devil and the antichrist, the guy who'd been in a position just like us – you remember him? He taught *me* what he knows, not you. He taught *me*. So it's *me* who has that burden."

His head shook, his nose curling upwards, his fists clenched.

"*Me*," he repeated.

"I miss Derek too," Oscar said. "But–"

"You didn't even know him."

Out the corner of his eye, Oscar saw April put her hand to her head and take a seat. He assumed she was shielding herself from the argument, but in truth, she had tuned out of the argument a while ago.

"Thea did something incredible today, Julian," Oscar persisted. "We should be celebrating that. It's a time of optimism, not a time for you to be arguing about authority."

"I'm not arguing. I'm telling."

"We should be working together!"

"Guys," April said, too quietly to be heard. Her eyes were closed and her hands were gripping her scalp.

"You know, Oscar, out of everything I've worked to create, you're the biggest disappointment."

"I'm not too fond of you either."

"Guys!" April shouted.

"And you know what–" Julian went to continue, but was interrupted by Oscar rushing to April's side.

"Are you okay?" Oscar asked.

"No…" April said.

"What is it?"

"Something's…something's happening… It's getting stronger…"

And, just as she said that, the phone rang, but as soon as Oscar answered it, the line went dead.

47

A SCREAM SHOOK ELIJAH, PROMPTING HIM TO DROP HIS PHONE. He picked it back up again to see that it had hung itself up.

"Damnit," he muttered.

In the distance, he saw nurses and doctors fleeing out of the psychiatric ward.

Between him and them was a long corridor, laid with bodies, much like the old lady he had just escaped. Some faced the corner and muttered, some lay catatonic on the floor – those were the ones that would usually scare him, but compared to the rest, they were the tame animals least likely to pounce.

He crept forward, startled by the sight of a man on the ceiling peering down at him, a wide-mouthed grin eating his cheeks, eyes that had turned vertically, a tongue that did not stop slashing blood.

Elijah didn't dawdle any longer.

He ran, only to be tripped up by a hand reaching out of an ajar door.

"Elijah!" beckoned the call of a doctor. "Come on, we're shutting up!"

He pushed himself to his feet and ran further on.

Gormless bodies meandered toward the open door, piling into clumps of empty vessels, blocking his way.

"Elijah, come on!"

He almost made it another few yards before something flew past his cheek and knocked him into the wall.

The phone was flung from his hand, disappearing beneath a mess of contorting creatures.

Bodies pushed themselves toward the crack of light in the main doors that had been left for Elijah. He was sure he could hear a vague apology before that light disappeared.

Disappeared.

The light from outside.

"My God…"

Have they trapped me in here?

Dragging himself to his feet, he looked beyond the bodies to find a shut door.

"No…"

He looked back to the lift.

It was surrounded by inhuman humans, moving like people shouldn't and hissing like people couldn't. He glanced over the mass of faces, looking for someone like him, a doctor, a nurse – or just someone who wasn't absently demented.

He was alone.

He opened the door to the nearest room, hoping to barricade himself in, but just slipped on the open stomach of messy body still dressed in scrubs, a toddler crouched over it with bloody smears across its cheek.

Suppressing a mouthful of sick, he turned back to the corridor, trying to plan his next evasive move.

That was when the lights went out.

Cackles and hisses and moans and croaking and rasping voices stung the air, filling him with a poisonous dread.

He tried edging himself across the wall, and regretted the

decision when his hand touched something soft. Something cold and fleshy. Something that preceded the clamping of a jaw around his wrist.

He screamed, and the surrounding assailants screamed mockingly after him. Like a monkey in a cage that made a noise so all the other monkeys imitated – except instead of monkeys, these were...

People.

God, they used to be people.

Now what?

He pulled himself away, gripping his wrist with his good hand, feeling warm liquid trickling between his fingers.

He rushed forward, no idea where he was going.

That's when he stopped trying.

What was there to do? Where was there to go?

He heard his phone ringing. Somewhere far off, somewhere unreachable, his ringtone of *Walking on Sunshine* announced an incoming call.

A hand around his throat told him his time was almost over.

All he'd ever wanted to do was help people.

Make sure they didn't suffer the torment he did as a teenager. Make sure the help they received for their mental health problems was better than he had. Make sure that...

It didn't matter now.

Something bit down on his neck and he let it happen.

He prayed they would do it quickly, that they wouldn't just bite him to death, that they wouldn't hack him to pieces, that someone would just snap his neck or slit his throat, something that may have greater initial pain but that would mean it was over soon.

He knew it wouldn't be over soon.

A dozen more mouths met his skin, pulling at various parts

of his body. The skin on his leg itched, his toe, his elbow, his face...

Oh, God, please, just let it be over...

Let it be over...

He closed his eyes and imagined being at home. In bed. Snuggled up to a beautiful partner, watching *X Factor* or some shit and pretending the world was okay.

The pain grew and he couldn't help but cry out, crying out for nothing and hating himself for it as it just seemed to spur them on.

A deeper bite into his throat destroyed his breath and he began to choke.

It was wildly unpleasant. Feeling his body trying to lurch for oxygen as his mind knew he'd never get it.

He was grateful; it would soon be over.

But it hurt. His mind swelled with multiple migraines as it began to shut down.

He closed his eyes and sank into death, greeting it like a friend he hated, but was grateful to find.

48

THE PHONE KEPT RINGING AND RINGING AND RINGING, BUT NO answer broke the attempt to call.

"Not answering," Oscar said. "Still not answering."

April kept her eyes closed, shielding herself from the light that was making her head throb.

"What is it, April?" Julian asked.

"I don't know," April answered. "I just – there's something, I don't know..."

"How do I find out the number?" Oscar asked.

"It's one four seven one, isn't it?"

"Get a pen and paper."

Julian grabbed a pen and pad from a nearby kitchen drawer. Oscar repeated the number as Julian wrote it down. He then took out his mobile and asked Julian to repeat the number back to him as he typed it into Google.

"Anything?" Julian asked.

"It's loading," Oscar replied as the search results revealed themselves. "It looks like a business number."

He scrolled down and clicked on it. It was the through number for a specific member of staff at...

His eyes closed. His head dropped.

No. Not again. Not there.

"What is it?" Julian pushed.

"It's the number for a mental health nurse at St. Helen's Psychiatric Unit. For Elijah, the guy who called us before."

No one spoke, but inside their minds, the same arguments batted back and forth.

What did this mean was happening?

Did they have to go back?

They couldn't. They had failed twice and lost...

A sixteen-year-old girl.

Losing her life.

Because of that place.

In the search results on his phone, something else caught Oscar's eye.

"Oh, God," he choked.

"What?"

He clicked on a link that led him to a BBC news page. The page was being updated live and the header read BREAKING NEWS.

"It's the BBC news page. It's the hospital, it..."

"What, Oscar? What is it?"

"It's being evacuated. They say that upwards of eight members of staff have lost their lives in an attack by the patients, and they are now barricading the remaining patients in."

"This is it," April said, massaging her temples.

"Then we have to go back," concluded Julian.

Oscar went to object but didn't. He wished to refute the statement but hated to do so. He took a seat and sat at the table, as did Julian. Confusion spread from one to the other, a conflict between the best of intentions and realistic aspirations.

"We can't," Oscar quietly spoke.

"We don't have a choice," April insisted. "People are dying."

"They've evacuated it now; the staff are fine."

"What about those still in? They may be possessed, but they are still human lives."

"Well, what are we supposed to do? How are we supposed to stop them?"

Julian sighed.

"Oscar's right," he concluded.

That was the last thing Oscar expected Julian to say.

"At least, partly," Julian added.

Ah. There it was.

"We can't just barge in there; we can't be reckless. Something needs to be done if people are dying – but we need to think about this carefully."

Oscar saw that April was still suffering, still rubbing her head, still facing downwards to avoid the light. He stood, poured her a glass of water, and placed it on the table before her.

"Thank you," she said, picking up the water and drinking it in sips.

"I agree we need to do something, but what if – what if we lose someone else? Like Thea?"

Julian nodded.

"I just – I don't know. I don't know what to do," Oscar admitted.

"Me neither," said April. "I can't face that place again."

A weighty absence of talk hung between them, words unsaid and unspoken. The three of them so distant from each other and the cause. Fear crippling their decisions, destroying their bravery.

They'd faced so much.

Been through Hell together.

And now…

"No," Oscar decided, shaking his head. "Then we can't. We can't go back. We just have to…"

"Let these people die?" Julian said, completing Oscar's question for him.

Oscar stood.

"I guess so," he said. "Like you said, sometimes we have to make sacrifices."

He solemnly left the room and made his way out of the front door, in a sudden desperate need for fresh air.

Was he committing these people to their death?

Was he making a logical, strategic decision that one may have to make in war?

Or, like he thought deep down, was he being the coward Julian so fervently believed he was?

He leant against the porch.

He knew the answer.

He knew it all too well.

THEN

APRIL ATE HER FOOD LIKE SHE'D NEVER EATEN BEFORE. A FEW weeks on the street, eating people's discarded pizza, using what little change was given to her to get a bottle of water and a chocolate bar, trying to convince herself she wasn't that hungry so her stomach pains would go away – all of this had left her ravenous.

She felt his eyes on her as she slurped spoonful after spoonful of soup, shovelling whole pieces of bread into her mouth. Her fingernails were dirty, but that had never made a difference on the street – dirty hands never made her sick. Cold nights and starving days bolstered one's immune system.

She didn't care if he was judging her, but she was sure he wasn't.

He'd said his name was Julian.

He'd said he knew why she heard the things she did, why she experienced the hallucinations she did.

Said they weren't even hallucinations.

Said he could help her.

What was she going to have to do in return?

RICK WOOD

"I'm not going to have sex with you," she stated, more bluntly than she'd intended.

"At no point was that my intention," Julian confirmed, his voice calm and steady, like he was trying to sound wise. "I just want to help you."

"No one helps anyone."

"That's not true."

"What is it you want?"

Julian exhaled his frustration. Maybe he wasn't after anything. Maybe he was just a good guy.

But good guys don't exist.

Take her father, for example.

The reason she ran away in the first place.

She used to dread bedtimes. Used to dread when it was her father's turn to read her a story. She used to lie in bed wondering why he did the things he did, why he needed to hold on while he read the book, like he was holding her hand, but worse.

She wondered if her mother knew.

It wasn't until they had sex education at school that she understood.

It wasn't until her mother didn't believe her that she thought maybe she was the one at fault; maybe she was prompting this.

Angry days after angry nights left her hostile. Fights at school never quelled the pain. Lonely lunches staring daggers at those who looked at her never endeared anyone to her, but she hated them all, their lies, their pretentious fakery, their facades, their perfect lives with their perfect faces laughing and mocking others they decided they didn't like.

She'd batted his hands away and he'd batted her face.

A swollen eye didn't convince her mother, she just asked, "Another fight at school again?"

She learnt to opt for silence.

230

Her second black eye prompted her to leave.

She doubted they even looked for her.

Good guys don't exist. People don't do things just to help others. This is not a Disney movie; this is reality – and, most of all, this was *her* reality.

She stopped eating and pushed the soup away.

"Did you not want to finish it?" Julian asked.

She glared at him, trying to decipher his undecipherable expression. He was so cool, his emotions so quelled. A performance the biggest psychopath in the world could be proud of.

"If you touch me, I'll bite your fingers off," she told him.

"I'm not going to touch you, April."

"Then why am I here? Why could you possibly want me here?"

"I want to help."

"People don't help!"

He leant forward and smiled. "I do."

She flinched away.

"How many girls do you pick up off the street?"

Julian sighed. He seemed offended by this. Like the suggestion was preposterous.

Yet the evidence directed her to the contrary.

"There are no strings attached," he persisted. "This is a home for you as long as you want it. You are a Sensitive. The things you see and hear, they are all part of it, and I want to help you. I want to guide you, to help you make the most of it."

"Why?"

"Because..."

He struggled at that question.

His face became entwined, like he was uncomfortable, working out a complex puzzle.

"Because it is my duty to do so."

"Your duty?"

"Yes. I am one too, and I want to recruit more, to help address the balance of Heaven and Hell."

Whoa.

This guy was a nutcase.

Alarms rang, sirens sounded; all in her mind, yes, but they made her alert.

"I'm going," she said, standing. "I'm not staying here with your sick delusions any longer. I've had enough."

She marched to the door.

"April, stop, please."

She placed a hand on the door handle.

"You are powerful."

She stopped. Looked over her shoulder. He stood across the hall, in the doorway to the kitchen, light from behind painting him in a neat silhouette.

"You are powerful beyond measure. More powerful than anyone could ever imagine. And I brought you here because I believe in you. If you wish to leave, then please, do; I'm not keeping you here. But if you wish to stay, and you wish to see just how powerful you are, then…"

He lifted his arms in a shrug and walked back into the kitchen.

April remained poised, her hand on the door handle, but making no effort to push it.

Powerful.

He said she could be powerful.

She thought about this.

And, as he sat in the kitchen, Julian hoped that, for once, he had said the right thing, and that he would no longer be alone in this fight.

NOW

50

THE LIVING ROOM FELT HEAVY. OSCAR, APRIL, SEB, AND THEA all sat around with a coffee, embracing a morning after no sleep. No one spoke and silence pursued, as it often seemed to. But this silence was worse.

It was a silence that covered the screaming of multiple patients mauling each other to death in St. Helen's Psychiatric Unit.

It was a silence that had existed too much – one of too many words unsaid.

It was a silence they all dreaded, but couldn't find any other way of communicating.

Julian entered the room.

Oscar covered his sneer. The last person he needed to bring the mood down even further. It seemed like Julian's sole purpose was to disagree with everything Oscar said.

But, as Julian had so clearly stated, *I am the one in charge.*

Oscar hadn't thought he was in charge, but with Julian sulking in the background for the last few weeks, he'd had no choice but to lead, had no choice but to step forward and speak to new people and encourage the new recruits.

Speaking to new people had been something that had always been scarier to Oscar than Hell, but it was an achievement that would always remain unspoken.

"This looks productive," Julian said, a slight grin wiping his cheeks.

Oscar rolled his eyes.

"I have decided what we are going to do," Julian declared. "I've made the decision, and, well…it's up to you all whether you wish to get on board, but it won't work without all of you."

"Does this decision involve you–"

"Now's not the time, Oscar. Now's the time for action. To stop squabbling and be bold."

Oscar's head slowly rotated toward Julian with the biggest glare he could give.

Stop squabbling?

Be bold?

How dare he!

"I know," Julian said, seeing Oscar's face and acknowledging his reaction. "I know, I know. But you need to listen with an open mind."

"My mind is wide open," Oscar responded. It wasn't.

"What is it, Julian?" April interjected, clearly attempting to defuse another heated debate that would end with nothing but hostility and indecision.

"We go back to St. Helen's."

Oscar scoffed.

"Hear me out," Julian persisted. "We have something we didn't have last time."

They all looked to Thea.

"Hey, I'm new here, I don't–"

"–Have any idea how powerful you are. And that is why you will go inside St. Helen's Psychiatric Unit."

Julian waited a beat for that to settle in before adding:

"Alone."

Oscar's jaw dropped. He was speechless. As if he hadn't rejected enough ludicrous suggestions, Julian came up with a far worse one.

"Isn't it bad enough we already lost one person?" Oscar asked.

"You lost someone?" Thea asked.

"You now want to put what may be our only hope on the firing line, alone, where they are killing each other?"

"They won't kill Thea," Julian declared.

"Why not?"

"Because they won't."

Oscar awaited further explanation but, as none was forthcoming, he threw his arms into the air and shook his head, unable to fathom what feasible reaction could convey his thoughts.

"That's not all," Julian continued. "The rest of us will go. All of us. And each one of us will take one of the four walls surrounding the unit."

"You want all of us to stand around the unit – alone?"

"Oscar, just listen."

Oscar closed his eyes and buried his face beneath his hand. He was beyond fuming.

"We attempt something that's never been attempted before. Something unprecedented, but something that I truly, truly believe will work."

"What?" April asked, seemingly willing to engage in Julian's ideas.

"A mass exorcism."

"A what?" Oscar retorted.

"We will surround the unit from all sides, each of us performing the Rites of Exorcism, each of us connecting with Thea as she enters."

"I don't know if I can do this," Thea said.

"Of course you can, Thea. With all of us performing the rites, all you have to do is walk in, channel that energy, and do what you did two nights ago."

"What did I do?"

"When you came to the house, when we were being attacked, you screamed out. As you did it, you released what you have – what Heaven gave you – and yesterday, you did it on a smaller scale. Now you simply have to control it. Control it, and release it, and with what we're doing we will–"

"Don't listen to him, Thea," Oscar said, standing, looking over the agape faces directed at Julian. "Nobody listen to him." He walked toward Julian. "I think it's time you thought about relocating."

"I'm not going anywhere."

"You're doing nothing but stirring up trouble. Putting ideas in people's heads."

"It's a bold move, Oscar, it is. But if we can do this, then maybe we can do a mass exorcism on a bigger scale, maybe that's how we–"

"How we what, Julian? Die? Fail miserably?"

"A risk is–"

"Not what we need right now, damnit!" He looked back at the people Julian's diatribe was harming, a tension he was making worse.

Had he completely lost his mind?

"Oscar, I know what I'm doing," Julian insisted, remaining calm.

"No, you don't, Julian. You truly don't."

"We all need to be in for this to work."

"Then it's not going to work."

With a lingering glare, Oscar kicked the door open and marched out. He made his way upstairs to his bedroom, much like he would have done when his parents told him off when he was a child – and he felt like a child, and that made him even angrier; that he was going back years to the person he used to be, back before he met April or…

He slammed the door behind him and leant against the wall.

He'd had enough.

51

JULIAN STEPPED OUTSIDE THE FRONT DOOR.

The evening air was cold, but that's why he'd stepped into it. He needed something to battle the dried perspiration, to reflect and consider.

To contemplate.

Derek would be disappointed with him, he was sure of it.

The wreck Julian had created…the Sensitives less together now than they'd ever been…

This was not what Derek had envisaged.

He leant against the porch. Bowed his head. Closed his eyes.

Tried to quieten his mind. To silence the shouts and listen to the quiet thoughts.

Oscar had screwed up.

He had screwed up big-time.

And Julian was hanging onto that. Clinging on, digging his fingers in and grasping onto the notion and not letting it go no matter what, no matter what Oscar did, April did, anyone did – Oscar was at fault for this entire mess.

And so what?

He shook his head.

No, he tried. He tried to separate himself from his anger, but he couldn't. It was too engrained in him, fixed in place as much as his heart, his liver, his veins – it was part of his body, with muscle built around it.

But one thought kept him from it, separated him from complete hostility and destruction:

What would Derek do in my position?

He'd tell Oscar he was a dick, that's for sure.

But he wouldn't put it that way.

It would be more like, "You're a damned fool, boy!"

Derek always had such thorough eloquence with words. Always so calm and patient. He kept his words to a minimum and remained thoughtful at all difficult moments.

Julian just opened his mouth and blurted out the most upsetting diatribe his irate mind could form.

What if Derek was still here?

Not ill as he once was, but instead, vibrant and full of energy. Pleased to help, eager to satisfy. He'd know what to do and say.

He'd know what the right words were and when the right time to use them was.

He turned back to the door and stopped. Turned the handle, then turned it back again.

What was he supposed to do? Just go in there and say sorry?

Oscar was a *damned fool.*

But Julian would be the *damned fool* if he let this go on without finding a way to bind them and unite them and drive them toward…

Toward what?

Delaying the inevitability?

They only stood a chance if they were together.

He dreaded to think what Seb thought. He wondered why Seb was even still there, what with the mess he'd entered. If it were Julian, he'd have run away long ago.

He took in a deep breath, held it, let it go.

They had something special now.

Thea.

But she needed a united support to achieve what Julian envisioned.

Derek wouldn't have let this happen.

Julian couldn't either.

He walked back into the house. Looked into the living room where Seb and Thea looked back at him, so vulnerable, so young.

We can't all stay young forever.

He turned away from them and made his way up the stairs.

APRIL QUICKLY FOUND HER WAY INTO THE BEDROOM TO FIND Oscar pacing, occasionally punching the wall, muttering, throwing his arms in the air as he ranted to himself.

"Oscar," she tried.

He stopped pacing and turned his visage of disbelief toward her.

"Can you believe that guy?"

"Oscar–"

"We've only just lost a teenage girl, and he wants to send another one in–"

April rushed up to him, putting her hands on his arms and looking into his eyes. She could tell almost instantly that her magical touch had cooled his boiling blood, had quelled his rage to simple frustration.

"Oscar, listen to me."

"I'm listening," he said – April probably being the only person he could honestly say that to.

"I think we should hear him out," she said, squeezing his arm tighter as he went to react. "Listen, Oscar, he's been a complete dick, I'm not arguing with you on that. But Thea has something, and I think it could work."

"Could work, April – *could* – work."

"We are running out of time. I can feel these things unlike you and Julian can, and I can feel it – every hour they grow stronger, every minute my mind is more overwhelmed. I can see it in Thea's eyes too. If we don't do something now, then we are going to lose any chance at all."

"But this?"

A few gentle knocks on the door heralded its opening. Julian stood in the crack.

"Mind if I come in?" he asked.

"That a joke?" Oscar said.

Julian forced a smile, entered, and closed the door behind him.

"You were right about one thing, Oscar," Julian stated. "We need to be together."

"You're realising this now?"

"You'll never get an apology from me, let me make that clear. It still stands that I think far less of you, that I'm still angry in a way that I can't stop."

Oscar turned to April to exchange a look of disbelief, to which she returned a raising of the eyebrows that told him to listen.

"But if we are to succeed, if we are to stand any chance at all – then you have to be an important part of that. You have to. And we can't do this without you." Julian stepped forward. "It's all or nothing."

April could see Oscar's thoughts racking his mind in a way no one else could. The subtle twitch of his eyes, the inter-changing curves of his frown, the tiny shakes of his head.

"We're together," Julian continued. "We're doing this together. It's the only way."

He stepped forward and extended his arm, his palm open for shaking.

"You have to be kidding me," Oscar said, putting his hands in the air to demonstrate his refusal.

"Oscar," April whispered. "This is his version of accepting he made a mistake."

"Then at some point of it he should probably accept that he made a mistake."

"I have," Julian said. "In not trusting you. I don't trust your judgement, but I trust your ability."

"Again, you suck at this."

Julian kept his hand held out, open, ready, waiting.

Oscar shook his head.

Julian returned his hand to his side and stood still for a few moments, gathering his words.

"Derek told me to recruit," Julian said. "He told me to gather those to fight this fight with me, to find other Sensitives. I try to be like him, but...he was forgiving and kind in a way I could never be."

Julian stepped forward and attempted a hand on Oscar's shoulder, one that made Oscar flinch away.

"I'm honest, and that's what I'm being."

April took Oscar's face in her hands and turned his toward hers.

"Trust me, Oscar," she told him. "This may not work. But if we don't do anything, then it's even worse."

Oscar took a huge intake of breath.

Julian extended his hand once again.

"What do you say?"

"You're a dick," Oscar said.

"Fair."

Oscar took Julian's hand and gave a brief handshake, as small a one as he could give, one that erred caution.

Julian nodded and backed away, leaving the room just after saying, "We leave in an hour."

Oscar turned to April and shook his head.

"You know he's only being nice to convince me," he said.

She said nothing. Instead, she leaned in, gave him a delicate kiss, one that lingered over his lips and made his body shake in that way she always could.

Then they exchanged those immortal words that would always exist between them no matter what:

"I love you."

"I love you, too."

CARNAGE CARRIED ITS MELODIC STRUGGLE THROUGHOUT THE depths of the corridors and corners of the rooms in St. Helen's Psychiatric Unit. Inside the smoky plaster holes and torn-apart walls of the facility was nothing resembling a peaceful place to care for the mentally ill.

It was more alike to a slaughter house. Except, in a slaughterhouse there is order, there is organisation, and reason behind the animals being killed for feeding.

Order and reason had long since departed.

Those few that were not suffering demonic possession and were genuinely ill witnessed the kind of sights that leave a lasting imprint on the scars of an impressionable memory. Even if they were to survive, the lasting images they endured would have only exacerbated their condition further.

One girl in particular, a teenager who had been discovered by her parents to have been self-harming and had admitted to a teacher she heard a voice telling her to do so, hid beneath a table. She regretted lying for attention; she regretted cutting for the sympathy. She regretted ending up where she was.

Attention was not worth this.

She stifled her breath, pushed a hand over her mouth and then the other, suffocating whimpers that seeped from her voice.

When the bloody splodge of a discarded heart landed on the floor before her, a fateful whimper found the cracks between her fingers.

A face before her, lined with fresh wounds, pale like the walls of her grandmother's kitchen, ducked down and smiled upon the sight of a fresh catch.

The girl turned and tried to slide away, but five fingers gripped one ankle and then the other, dragging her out like a gurney.

They didn't suffer her the indignity of immediate death. They indulged her in the possibility of survival before reaching their hand so far down her mouth they could see the outline of their fingers pushing against the skin of her throat.

More of the possessed appeared, smelling the skin of a touched body, and fought against her original assailant for the pleasures of her company.

Fresh surgical equipment came welded into the palm of one such happy camper, and they decorated her like tinsel haphazardly applied to a cheap Christmas tree. By the time they had finished, the only thought that remained was how her parents would no longer be able to identify her face to the police.

To make matters worse, they pulled out her teeth by the dried skin of their fingers.

A hasty decision prompted her to grab the wrist of the hand entwined with the surgical equipment so recklessly left discarded in the room of a feverish mind, and she pushed the scalpel into her throat, giving her the desperate but brief pain of suffering that would lead to her grateful death.

Once the genuinely ill and those unmolested by demons had gone, they turned on each other. Feeding on the weaker amongst them, the younger that attempted to inherit the earth but held too loose a grip on their victim.

The demons never died, but the bodies they inhabited were torn up and left to shreds.

The purpose was not infiltration, but to incite fear. These attacks weren't isolated; they were occurring across the Earth.

Their permanence would be made apparent once the fear was heightened.

They were released. Liberated. Running amok amongst men with enlightened violence left in their wake.

No one could stop them now.

No one.

FIVE FIGURES APPROACHED THE EXTERIOR OF ST. HELEN'S Psychiatric Unit, quite unable to comprehend the mess it had become.

Doors and windows were sealed with planks of wood and police barricades. A perimeter was formed with fences. Outside of this were ambulances seeing to doctors and nurses and cafeteria workers and caretakers and visitors and any other poor soul who had been unfortunate enough to have been there.

Police stood idly, watching the building.

A van arrived and a set of riot police stepped out, arming themselves with helmets and shields.

"They are going to send the riot police in," Oscar noted.

"What will the riot police do?" Seb naïvely asked.

A glance from Oscar gave no need to answer the question.

"Oh…"

"We haven't much time," Julian stated.

He turned to the others.

April looked back at him, a look of vulnerability; the same one he saw in her face the first time he ever saw her. Nostalgia came over him and he suddenly wished they were back in his first flat, him teaching her what she was, watching her grow to trust him, feeling a bond that would prove unbreakable.

He looked to Oscar. A foolish child but a strong Sensitive. A person attempting to right his wrongs, probably more so than Julian had given him credit for.

Seb. A boy growing into a young man Julian could learn to trust. A stupid, hormonal child growing into a strong, potential warrior for the cause.

And Thea. The saviour. The one they were throwing into the front line and hoping for the best.

He prayed this decision wasn't going to backfire on him.

"Do we all have what we need?" he asked.

All but Thea opened their bags and checked their items:

The Rites of Exorcism.

Rosary.

Holy water.

Candle.

Salt.

And, most importantly, the crucifix.

"Then we're ready," he concluded.

Looking back over those faces once more, he grew a sense of pride.

Derek had asked him to gather those like him, to lead them, to have a group of Sensitives.

He hoped Derek was looking upon him with pride.

"I'm honoured to be doing this with you all," Julian said, smirking at the surprise on Oscar's face. "I'm not going to say may God be with us all, because I've yet to see him on this journey. All I'll say is, stay safe. We can do this."

More riot police arrived. It was time.

"Thea," Julian prompted. "When you're ready."

She stepped forward.

Closed her eyes. Took a deep intake of breath. Loosened her

hands, removed any tension in her body – just as April had taught her – and opened her eyes once more.

She ran.

Ran past the gathering riot police, ran past the ambulance. Approaching a caretaker with his back to her, she held her hand out and grabbed hold of his keys, yanking them off his belt and disappearing past him before he could realise what had happened.

She leapt upon the fence.

"What's she doing!" came one of the many yelps behind her.

She heard them running, but she had climbed the fence and approached the building before they had even managed to comprehend the fact that a teenage girl was attempting to enter the facility.

"Don't go in there!" she heard one doctor scream. "It's not safe!"

She tossed aside the police barricade and put the keys in the lock.

Glancing over her shoulder, she saw that no one had bothered to climb the fence to get her.

Even law enforcement were too scared. They were only prepared to enter with helmets and shields and batons and in greater numbers.

She would have to rely on far less than that.

She turned the lock, entered, shut the door behind her, and locked it from the inside.

Julian, Oscar, April, and Seb watched the commotion outside, the uproar of disbelief and worry as to what had just happened.

"That's our cue," Oscar said.

He and April shared a kiss and a hand squeeze that Julian was sure they thought no one else noticed, and they departed.

"If it's all right with you," Julian joked, looking to Seb. "I don't think we should kiss."

"That's fine with me," Seb said, grinning back at him.

Seb left for his side of the building.

Julian remained at the front.

He kissed his crucifix and went to his knees, preparing the ritual.

April finished watching Oscar leave, then looked back at Julian, already in his own world.

Then she looked to the door to St. Helen's, now closed, Thea inside it.

Thinking of the words she'd said to her. The instructions, the encouragement.

Hoping it was enough.

Praying it would do.

THIRTY MINUTES AGO

55

THEA, LISTEN TO ME.

You might think you are just a girl.

Just a teenager.

A runaway.

But so was I, Thea. So was I.

I struggled against all the things I heard, all the things I saw. Everywhere I looked, it seemed like there was another mask of violence looking my way.

They spoke to me, made me think I was crazy.

I was not crazy, Thea.

You are not crazy either.

This is who you are.

And it is your ability to embrace who you are that gives you strength.

For me, Julian showed me that strength, and Oscar reinforced it – every day I rely on those two and have no idea what I would do without them.

See that strength in me.

We have only just met, but we've been there all along.

I saw you in the woods. I saw you before that. I saw that struggle.

I saw that power, but I also saw much more.

Inside of you, there is anger.

Not just at your brother, whom you miss dearly; that is clear for everyone to see.

Not just at the world for the way this burden has been inflicted on you.

But at yourself, for being that person.

And I could tell you that you shouldn't be angry, that you shouldn't feel hard-done by, that you shouldn't feel under pressure, and everyone will tell you that and tell you that and tell you that until you can't take them saying it any more.

But it's not the truth.

I will tell you the truth, Thea.

It is okay to feel that way.

It is okay to feel mad at your brother for letting that demon in, for destroying your family, for taking himself away from you.

It is okay to be mad at the world because you are the one who has had to do this; you are the one who we've asked to undertake such a great task so soon.

But, most of all, my dear, dear Thea – it is okay to be angry at yourself.

People think emotions are something to quell, something to keep down.

You are a Sensitive.

Emotions give you power.

I feel the emotions of the spirit I'm channelling and that is how I control them.

Enter that unit, feel the hate, feel the anger, feel the death that surrounds you. Acknowledge the violence, acknowledge the mayhem, and acknowledge that it is okay that it upsets you.

That it angers you.

Because you are a gift to this world, Thea.

A truly wonderful gift.

And I'm so glad I met you.

So when you get in there, give them hell, and know I believe in you.

Not because of who you are and what you can do.

But because I know you are angry.

I know you are human.

And that is what will give you focus.

We will be counting on you, but you will be counting on us, too.

I will not let you down.

And I will see you afterwards, where I will give you a big hug and help you to be reunited with your parents, help explain to them what you are, what you can do.

This world is horrible, Thea.

But you aren't.

Good luck.

Now go and show them why Heaven chose to give this gift to you.

NOW

56

ONE FOOT PLACED PRECISELY BEFORE THE OTHER, STEPPING OVER pools of blood and discarded carnage.

The sight made Thea's breakfast lurch to her throat.

She resisted the temptation to be scared by the sight, to let it get to her, to let it push her into fear.

She had nothing to fear.

In the blackness she could make out rapid movements of figures, grappling outlines of bodies. The sounds were growing with every step – biting, hissing, growling, groaning, croaking – every inhuman sound that could be pushed through a human throat, surrounding her. From behind her, from distant doors, even from above.

She withdrew a torch Julian had given her and flicked the switch.

Its illumination only gave her sparse images. She waved the light around, seeing the wide, startled eyes of a feral human clinging to the wall with all fours, the inside out body of a man without a face, the struggling body coming toward her dragging a broken leg left twisted behind them.

The stench hit her next. Like rotting meat left out for days.

Like decayed vegetables and expired milk and infected skin left untreated.

They crept toward her, displaying caution, taken aback by the bizarre image of a teenage girl bracing the lost facility.

She flicked the torch between approaching faces.

Each advancing body moved in a uniquely unnatural way. Some were like predators moving like a lion upon its prey. Some moved with their joints dislocating on every action. Some slithered along the floor, pushed by their feet like a demented lizard.

That sickly feeling in her stomach grew.

All that telling her not to be afraid proved useless.

Between and behind each of these oncoming scarred and repulsive faces were bodies, blood, leftovers. Not just victims but tortured souls, ripped to an unrecognisable clutter.

She didn't want to die, nor did she want to be torn into pieces.

She didn't imagine they'd wait for her life to be over to begin transforming her into a bloody mess.

"Oh, God…" she choked upon the sight of another body with slashes across their face, wounds left open by the crust of dried blood.

Why am I doing this…

Her life before was awful, it was far from ideal – but it was nothing like this.

How had she let those crazy people talk her into this?

She realised she was holding her breath, but she didn't release it. It caught somewhere between her throat and her mouth.

Invisible locusts twisted inside her gut.

She looked over her shoulder.

The door was way down the other end of the corridor, but could she still make it? If they decided to pounce, could she still make it?

Bodies crawling from rooms either side of the door blocked her passage and told her *no*.

The only way out of this was to believe their delusions.

April had believed it.

April had been so sure of it.

How had April known her if it wasn't true? If she couldn't do something about this? If she had no way of–

One of them leapt forward, landing at her feet. As it looked up at her its head twisted, turning to an unnatural position, hanging from its back the wrong way.

She instinctively kicked its head but it was not deterred.

She held out her hand.

Its jaw opened, revealing blackened gums and bloody teeth.

It pounced.

"No," she unknowingly stated.

She held out her hand and the advancing assailant was flung backwards.

It did not deter the others, who continued to approach.

57

As Seb took to his knees, feeling them sink into the soft grass, he realised his arms were trembling.

Why? Why were they trembling?

It was a simple procedure. He'd been given clear instructions; he could remember them with perfect clarity.

And, besides, he wasn't the one entering the hive of violence.

This was for Thea. He'd found it hard enough being plunged into a world he'd never known of – she was being plunged even farther, even sooner.

No, can't think about the stakes.

Can't get distracted.

Just have to concentrate on what I'm doing, make sure I get that right.

He took the salt and poured a large quantity into his hand. He tipped his hand slightly to let out a small trickle of salt, then moved his hand around himself to spread the salt until it surrounded him in a full circle.

This will protect you, Julian had said. *This is what will keep you safe.*

The last of the salt left his hand, creating a full, unbroken circumference.

Right. That was that. What was next?

Ah, the holy water.

He pressed the tips of his forefinger and middle finger against the end of the flask, tipped slightly, and felt his fingers dampen. Placing the flask by his side, he took his damp fingers and used them to create a cross over his body.

The holy water is another form of protection, Julian's voice reminded him. *Use it like war paint, displaying your colours to the enemy.*

Strange, really; a few days ago he was an atheist and would mock people doing such ridiculous things. And, to be honest, he probably still would – his atheist beliefs had been based on lack of evidence and now, if anything, he was overwhelmed by proof.

He withdrew three candles. He placed one in front of himself, one by his left foot and one by his right.

The candles will form the holy trinity, Julian had said. *Your final layer of protection. We cannot be too cautious when we are going up against an evil so strong.*

He lit them, then tucked the lighter back in his pocket.

The final step, the rosary – which he withdrew and placed around his neck.

He was supposed to kiss the crucifix at the end of the rosary. He felt immensely stupid doing so, but did so anyway, following Julian's instructions to the letter.

An exorcism demands faith; show it.

Finally, he withdrew the Rites of Exorcism.

This was it.

The book that had the prayers they would all need to attack this thing.

His defence was prepared; now for the words.

He closed his eyes. Held a breath.

He could run. He could get up and sprint, get out of there, leaving them all to it. Refuse to be part of it.

What if he ended up like Maddie?

Then again, no. That wasn't who he was now.

He opened his eyes and opened the book.

"Holy Mother of God, Holy Virgin of virgins," he began.

He paused. Sighed.

What was he doing?

He wiped a bead of sweat from his brow.

He silently hoped that Thea was still alive.

Then, pushing all reluctance from the forefront of his thoughts, he persevered.

"All holy angels and archangels, all holy orders of blessed spirits," he continued.

58

A UNIFIED DIAMOND ENCOMPASSED ST. HELEN'S PSYCHIATRIC Unit.

From one side, Oscar.

Knelt in his circle of salt and triangle of candles like the others – not something they normally did, but extra protection they felt was needed.

"For haughty men have risen up against me and fierce men seek my life."

He'd said the words a hundred times without ever giving them a second thought. He was reading the words of the Rites of Exorcism and, as far as he was concerned, he could be reading a menu for a Chinese takeaway or the lines in a bad school play.

What had always mattered to Oscar was that they worked.

But, in a strange kind of unconscious reflection, he spoke the words and listened to them.

Haughty men have risen up against me.

Haughty was a word he hadn't heard many times, but believed it to mean arrogantly superior – something demons believed they were.

Seek my life.

These Hell-dwellers sought not only his life, but the lives of everyone he had met, is yet to meet, and will never meet – all life on this Earth was there with the predicament of being potentially disposed of.

They sought their lives in order to remove them and inherit the Earth once more.

Oscar stated the rest with resolve, determination, a definite understanding that he would not let the demons have what they wished for.

"God, by Your name save me and by Your might, defend my cause."

From the next side, April.

These words were new to her.

Her gift was as a conduit, to channel the spirit or pick up on the demon.

She'd assisted in exorcisms before, but as someone who gave a response – never as the speaker of the words.

Now here she was, learning new skills. Her role changing. Ready to take on the challenge if it meant having any possibility of saving the world.

"For haughty men have risen up against me and fierce men seek my life."

She detected a quiver in her voice and reassured herself she was reading the correct words.

This was not a time to be scared of words, to be fearful of reciting prayers. After all, that was all they were – words.

New or not, her job was simple.

Stay within the circle of salt, stay within the candles, and recite the rites with deadset accuracy.

"God, by Your name save me and by Your might, defend my cause."

She closed her eyes, took a moment.

Tried to listen for Thea, feel for her, tried to see if she was doing okay.

To see if she was still alive.

A stark realisation of the task they'd set upon her and the war zone they'd sent her into hit her like a wayward brick across an unsuspecting face.

Stop it; no time for fear.

Time for bravery.

Time for strength.

She looked at the next line and recited it perfectly.

From the next side, Seb.

Gaining more and more confidence the more he spoke.

All he was doing was saying words.

It wasn't that hard.

He didn't stumble over syllables or falter over conjunctives. He articulated them with immense precision.

It felt odd.

This should be tougher.

"For haughty men have risen up against me and fierce men seek my life."

Prayers.

Words.

Talk.

"God, by Your name save me and by Your might, defend my cause."

It was cheap.

As he read the words he prayed in his mind – *Thea, you got this.*

And he hoped she was okay.

At the final side, Julian.

With eyes on the cluster of vans dispersing riot police, readying themselves to gain entry, to charge in and split up the mayhem.

They may be surprised at what they find.

"That You spare us, that You pardon us, that You bring us true penance and that You govern and preserve Your holy Church."

He closed his eyes.

He could say these words without the book.

If Thea was dead, it would all mean nothing.

But he couldn't think like that. He was strong.

He just hoped the rest were being as strong.

"That You preserve our Holy Father and all ranks in the Church and holy religion."

He paused, watched the riot police getting into formation, and added to his prayer:

"I believe in you, Thea. Come on."

59

THEY APPROACHED IN A CLUSTER TOWARD HER, ENTWINING THEIR limbs in disjointed movements.

Another leapt toward her.

Thea raised her hand and said, "No."

The figure attempting to strike her – she couldn't even tell if it was man or woman or beast anymore – fell back.

She closed her eyes.

For haughty men have risen up against me and fierce men seek my life.

The words soared through her like a drug in her veins, spreading authority throughout her body.

She felt it tingle her toes, rush through her calves and bolster her thighs. Her belly disarmed the locusts and butterflies, replacing them with steel, forming a strength she had never felt before.

She lifted her arms out to the side, forming her own crucifix, although she had not consciously made the decision to do so – she could *feel* it.

Heaven.

She could feel Heaven flooding through her, feel what was

inside her, what had conceived her. Her stiffening arms grew in invisible muscle, her throat turned and her head, facing above, grinned as her eyes closed and she relished the passionate sting of hope.

More descended on her, but she didn't even need to move to thrust them backwards.

God, by Your name save me and by Your might, defend my cause.

She could hear their words in unison echoing around the theatre of her mind. She could feel the vibration of their voices, the determination with which they spoke their words designed to empower her.

And empowered she was.

No longer did they approach her, or crawl toward her, or hiss or leer or groan or croak or scream or attempt any kind of attack or intimidation.

The intimidation had reversed.

She could feel their confusion, unable to understand.

Who was this girl?

What was she doing?

How was she doing it?

Feeling their next verse booming over her, she spoke it with them.

"That You spare us, that You pardon us, that You bring us true penance and that You govern and preserve Your holy Church."

Her voice grew stronger, grew womanlier, more fluid, and she could feel it projecting over the entire facility without strain or ease – just the divine speech of her divine voice.

"That You preserve our Holy Father and all ranks in the Church and holy religion."

She stepped forward.

She didn't need to open her eyes to see them flinch, see them scatter away from her.

The death, the violence, the sadistic cruelty inflicted on the innocents.

These were the innocents.

And with that thought, she heard the words spoken by a single voice, Julian's voice, definite, a prayer said just for her.

I believe in you, Thea. Come on.

Feeling divine influence pouring through her, something more than adrenaline, something invigorating her veins, the celestial throb of her open palms, the deity within her – she opened her eyes.

It was time to end this.

She pointed her hand at the nearest victim of possession and watched as the demon struggled, writhed, moaned, and fled through the innocent's mouth and plunged downwards with a screech.

"TURN BACK THE EVIL UPON MY FOES AND IN YOUR faithfulness, destroy them," Julian recited, dropping the Rites of Exorcism to the ground and rising to his feet.

He didn't need it.

And he could feel it. Strength pushing through, pursuing.

Was it possible this was actually working?

"Because from distress You have rescued me, and my eyes look down upon my enemies."

Riot police approached the door in perfect formation, two clear lines approaching the front.

Edging, cautiously placing one foot forward and shuffling the other behind.

The Rites of Exorcism were nearly at their end.

"Who ascended into Heaven and sits at the right hand of God the Father Almighty, from there He shall come to judge both the living and the dead."

He could hear his voice growing stronger, confidently louder.

Doctors and paramedics began to turn to look at him.

He smiled. It didn't matter. It was already done.

"And those who have done good," Julian continued, his voice conclusive, "shall enter into everlasting life, but those who have done evil into everlasting fire."

He sighed.

"As it was in the beginning."

And it was done.

He waited.

The instructions he gave were not to leave your circle until they saw Thea again, until they could clearly see her whole, empowered body walking out of the building with a face beaming with success.

But she was not forthcoming.

He felt like it was working, yet she had not walked out.

For a brief moment, something occurred to him.

His circle of protection. It had been broken.

There was a gap in the circumference of salt.

One of his candles blew out.

He thought nothing of it, and resumed his focus on Thea – not realising how catastrophic this would prove to be.

A thunderous crashing caused Julian to shield his face. Once his arm had dropped, he looked back to the windows, all of which had been shattered.

Was this good, or was this bad?

He didn't know.

So he did the only thing he knew.

"Derek," he spoke, quietly, a prayer just of his own. "Please hear me. Please be watching over."

Riot police retreated a few metres, covering their faces.

They waited, then they continued to proceed.

"I trust in you as you trusted in me."

Broken glass cracked beneath dozens of heavy boots.

"Please give her strength. Please help us."

THEN

DESPITE BEING IN PRISON, DESPITE SITTING IN THE MEETING room amongst many family members despairingly talking to their convicted loved ones, despite the weaker shade of life pressed against Derek's face – his calm, steady eyes of reason still persisted in the way they always had.

"He's reckless," Julian complained.

"You said the same thing about April when you met her."

"At least she had good cause to be reckless. She lived on the street – what's *his* excuse?"

Derek grinned – not a showing off in-your-face grin, but a knowledgeable grin, one that showed he was thinking far deeper thoughts than anyone else could know.

"I could have said the same thing about you when we first met," Derek observed.

"No – I was at least focussed, not just trying to get into some girl's pants."

"He likes April, then?"

"Oh, God, it's obvious. They'll be the death of each other, I'll tell you that."

"What's wrong with them falling in love?"

"What's right with it? There's a bigger cause; love distracts."

"Sometimes people need something to fight for."

"Why are you always being so obtuse?" Julian threw his arms into the air. "For once, just stop contradicting me with these bullshit statements designed to make me think; for once just acknowledge what I'm thinking and agree."

Derek momentarily dropped his head, biting his lip. He hung his head like it had been dropped by the hangman before lifting it again moments later.

"You need to be better than this," Derek said.

"What?"

"Do you think I had the time to complain? Do you think I didn't worry that Levi, Eddie, you – that you all didn't come with your faults."

"And what's your fault, Derek?"

Derek chuckled, raising his arms and looked around the room to indicate where he was.

"Look at where this path has led me. I'm in prison for trying to exorcise a girl and failing. That is the punishment for not being perfect."

"You did all you could."

"But in my mind, it will never be enough. I deserve to be here."

"No, you don't."

"I lost a girl, Julian."

"*We* lost a girl."

"You were my apprentice; there was no responsibility on you."

"But failure doesn't mean you deserve to be locked away."

"It is the price I pay."

"And what about when Oscar fails, huh? When April fails? When their love proves to be the death of us all, what happens then, huh? Am I supposed to sit back and look all calm and wise like you, or am I supposed to sit there, sarcastic-clapping, telling them I told you so because that's what a jerk like me does?"

Derek let Julian's outburst hover between them, letting the words settle, letting them dissolve.

"You're angry," Derek said.

"I'm always angry."

"But more so."

"I just – I don't have the temperament you do, Derek. I don't suffer fools as well as you."

"Hah!" Derek blurted out without meaning to.

"What's so funny?"

"I once heard a lyric in a song, I don't remember what song it was, but it said – the real you is who you are when no one's watching."

"What's your point?"

"You saw the me you needed to. Nothing more. Nothing less."

"So you felt frustrated?"

"Every damn day."

This rendered Julian speechless. When you idolise someone, place them on such a pedestal, create such a strong mentor figure, it is hard to see them as anything but impenetrable. But, in the end, we all are. However much we seem not to be.

"So what did you do?" Julian asked. "When you felt frustrated?"

"Reminded myself."

"Reminded yourself of what?"

"What the cause was."

"It's the cause that's–"

"And what I could control."

"What?"

Derek sighed.

"I reminded myself of what I could control and what I

couldn't. And I let what I couldn't control go, then took action about what I could."

"But how do you just let something go?"

"Time!" shouted the prison officer.

Derek forced a reluctant smile. This conversation wasn't finished at the point either Julian or Derek wanted it to finish.

"I advise patience," Derek said.

"Patience?"

"You have got what I never had. I had an antichrist and a lecture theatre. You have actual people conceived by Heaven."

"But it's not–"

"Julian, you have the opportunity here to do something remarkable. Something amazing. With the other Sensitives with you, and being led by you, and at their best – you can do things I could never have imagined. Fight Hell in the way I never thought possible."

"It's too tough."

"A burden is always tough when you see it as a burden, not an opportunity."

A prison officer appeared at Derek's side and he stood.

"Do something incredible, Julian. Something I never could. Something I never dreamt possible."

And before Julian could say another word, Derek was taken away and Julian was left alone with his thoughts.

NOW

THE BODIES COLLAPSED BEFORE THEA LIKE A GREAT FLOOD.

One grabbed onto their hair as they squirmed and wiggled against their bodily imprisonment.

Another coughed of mouthful of bloody vomit, black juice oozing out.

Another seized on the floor like a dying worm, its fingers pointed and its legs uncontrollable.

Thea simply stood, held her arms outward, waving them over the faces before her. She watched agape as they changed, transformed, transfixed by her gift.

When she finally dropped her arms to her side, she was able to witness the glorious mayhem and diabolical magnificence she had caused.

The pale faces grew red, contorting bodies grew limp, crawling bodies lay down.

She felt a spark of quiet disbelief. A knowledge she'd always had that she could do this, but a recognition that she'd never actually expected to see it.

These people were safe.

Because of her.

Because of *Thea Kinsey*. A nutjob from Worcester.

The door burst open and in came the riot police. Punching through to every room, shouting, clearing the area, ready for battle.

But they did not find a battle.

They found faces awakening from a tormented sleep. People who had taken a backseat to their bodies finding their skin once again, filling their bodies with their soul, opening their eyes and seeing the world for themselves.

Some retributed victims looked at her, astonished; some looked at her afraid. But most looked at her with grateful servitude.

She turned and walked through the armed police, who fled through the facility, finding a tranquil scene they did not expect.

She smiled as she sauntered past their halted confusion, their immense surprise at a situation solved.

A few of them turned to each other and questioned, *Is this it?*

A few continued searching the building, sure they would find something.

They wouldn't.

Thea had seen to that.

These souls had been freed.

She left them to it, gliding out of the building.

6 3

AT THE FIRST SIGHT OF HER EXITING THE BUILDING, JULIAN DREW out his phone and sent a group text:

IT'S SAFE. She's here.

SEB WAS the first to appear at his side. Julian planted a hand on his shoulder.

"Your first exorcism completed," Julian stated. "How do you feel?"

Seb was too exhausted to answer coherently. He simply smiled and let out a sigh of relief, which prompted Julian to chuckle.

April appeared at his side next, a wide grin spread beautifully across her face. He opened his eyes and suffocated her in a hug, a hug that she eagerly reciprocated. They laughed, chuckling heartily at their achievement.

Finally, Oscar was the last to return.

His expression looked grim, concerned. Julian grew instantly wary.

"What is it?" Julian asked, worried about what Oscar may be about to say.

"I – I–" Oscar stuttered. "I – I just can't believe it worked."

Julian grinned, a grin which Oscar returned.

Julian offered his hand, which Oscar took, and they gripped tightly, shaking heartily, laughter surrounding their joy.

Oscar then turned to April and took her in his arms and kissed her like he meant it.

"If it's all right with you," Julian said to Seb, "I think we'll veto the kissing."

"I think that's fine," Seb returned.

Then, finally, Thea approached. Wiping sweat from her brow, dragging her legs like boulders were attached.

She fell to her knees as she approached and April rushed to her side, putting her arms around her.

Thea lifted her head, wiping tears from her cheeks.

It was at this point they all realised what she may have seen in there. What she may have had to face, had to dodge, had to witness.

"Oh my God, are you okay?" April said. "Talk to me, Thea, come on. Are you all right?"

Thea's weary, distraught face moulded into a weak smile.

"It worked," she spoke, so weakly they had to listen hard to decipher it. "It...it worked..."

"It did," April confirmed. "It really did. You were amazing. You really were."

"I can't believe it..."

"Can you stand? Come on."

April helped her to her feet.

"We need to get her some rest," she said to the others.

"We will," Julian confirmed. "But first, I think we need to see this."

In the time since they had finished the ritual, more people had amassed outside the hospital. Civilians.

Families.

From the door, they emerged. Some with their arms around a man in riot gear, some staggering out as they collapsed against the wall, some pushing themselves up from the floor to their feet.

All of them wounded, meek, hurt.

But all of them free.

All of them liberated from the demonic confines inflicted upon them.

Upon recognising a face, a family would flee to them, would push aside the parted fence and grab their loved one with all they had.

More paramedics arrived and wounds were treated. Slashes across faces were dabbed with cotton and gashes in calves were wrapped with bandages and broken legs left dangling behind those who limped were put into cast.

More families came and more were reunited.

Julian crouched beside Thea, placing a hand on her shoulder.

"Look at this," Julian said, directing her fading gaze toward the scenes below.

"What?" Thea asked.

"You did this, Thea," Julian told her. "You did this."

And, despite her need to rest and a burning craving for sleep, she watched with the rest of them.

"We need to get her some rest," April insisted.

"We will, I promise," Julian answered. "But first, let her watch this. Let her see."

Julian wanted her to revel in her success, to watch the love and retribution and joy being displayed in the scenes below.

Together, they watched.

All of them.

The Sensitives.

Standing together, victorious, with hope they would never have foreseen.

TWO DAYS LATER

The weight of positivity is always measured by the negativity that follows.

The day after the success at St. Helen's Psychiatric Unit was a day of celebration, of success. A toast to the first battle won, a marvel at what they had achieved, and astonishment at what this could mean in terms of potential, of things to come.

But, following the celebrations, Oscar, April, and Julian were alone as the others slept, and reality battered down the door once more.

"We know it's still small, though," Julian had pointed out.

Oscar was tempted to roll his eyes; typical Julian, always looking to spoil the party and bring everyone plummeting back down to earth.

But this time, he didn't.

Because Julian was right.

"I know," Oscar acknowledged.

"I mean, what happened was incredible – but it was one building. One building in a whole world."

"I think the celebration isn't a presumption that we've won,"

April said, "but a celebration of what we can do. This is bigger than anything we've done before. This means that we could, maybe, do it on an even bigger scale."

"But we don't know that, do we?" Julian had insisted. "We know we can take it from, I don't know – one percent to three percent. But does that mean we can take it from three percent to one hundred?"

An uncomfortable silence ensued as the room awaited Oscar's protestations, but they didn't come.

"You're right," Oscar said. "What we did was incredible, but it's still small. We're still far off where we need to be."

Oscar stood, pouring himself a glass of water in a small tumbler and drinking it all in one.

"We need to stop sitting around talking about how great it was," Oscar said, "and begin looking at how we can do it again, but even bigger."

"Can a mass exorcism even be done on a bigger scale?" April mused.

"No," Julian said. "I've looked into it, and it doesn't appear so. Even with Thea, we can't do a whole world in one go."

"Then we do it bit by bit," Oscar suggested. "We find the hot spots and we go there, and we do it."

"Then we need to find the hot spots," Julian agreed.

"I think the news would be the best place to start," April said.

With that, they began researching. They found multiple places with multiple slaughters, and promptly grew overwhelmed by the scale of disaster the world was facing.

And, like that, they were brought straight back into reality.

A reality that was disrupted by a knock on the front door.

Oscar answered, and there stood three scared-looking people. A girl and two boys. Wet from the rain and looks of terror spread from ear to ear.

"Father Lorenzo Romano sent us," one of them volunteered. "He said you would know who we are."

Oscar couldn't help but smile. It would have been nice for the Vatican to provide them with some warning!

He let them in and found them a space in the living room. By the time he'd been to the local outdoors shop and returned with three sleeping bags, five more had arrived.

Over the next few days, more kept coming.

Julian carried on the search for places to target, April taught the conduits techniques, and Oscar went over the Rites of Exorcism with the wide-eyed raised-eyebrow faces of the spritely new recruits.

They had an army, but an army with no experience.

Oscar and April still slept in their room together, but every other room were given bunk beds, funded by the Vatican and put together by Seb and whatever other idle Sensitive he could find to help him.

Every night, Oscar kept his arms around April as they fell asleep. Once he turned over, she followed, and placed her arms around him. They held each other tight, starkly aware of the possibility they may not see old age together as they had always planned.

They were always anxious about the war, stressed about the next battle, but exhaustion prevented their overactive minds from preventing their sleep.

That is, apart from one night when Oscar lay awake with his eyes still open. April, breathing heavily behind him, still held him tight in her sleep.

He had so many sporadic thoughts, so many notions he went over, so many concerns.

There was little he was sure of nowadays.

The only definite thought Oscar had was that something had changed.

And, although the war was far from won, at least there was unity.

At least there were the Sensitives.

And, most importantly, at least there was hope.

65

JULIAN HADN'T TOLD ANYONE.

He'd kept it to himself.

Didn't want the concern. Didn't want the worry.

No need to alarm anyone. He'd been doing this long enough. He could deal with it himself.

But there had been a break in his circle. A gap in the salt. And a candle had gone out.

Something had entered that circle.

And that something hadn't left.

And that something had attached itself to him, had found its way inside. Something lingering from the psychiatric unit, something...

Something that was gripping him from the inside, taking control, denying him the opportunity to speak honestly about it.

He'd hid it at the time.

Now it wouldn't let him say anything. It wouldn't let him form the words.

He stumbled out of bed. Looked at the clock.

It was 3.00 a.m. on the hour.

Supposedly the witching hour. The time when the paranormal was at its strongest.

It meant nothing.

It was just a time.

Get up, Julian. Get up.

He stepped from his bed and made his way into the bathroom, opening the cabinet and searching out a pack of paracetamol. He pushed two out, put them in his mouth, and drank water straight from the tap.

Two won't be enough.

He pushed out every pill from the packet and counted them in twos.

Two. Four. Six. Eight. Ten. Twelve. And one more.

That made thirteen.

He put all of them in his mouth, drank straight from the tap and swallowed. It felt like a lot of bumps pushing down his throat, and his stomach gurgled in response.

It's still not enough.

What else did it want?

He looked through the rest of the medicines. He found a pack of sertraline. Antidepressants he assumed had been Maddie's.

"Is this enough?" he asked.

He had no answer, so he tried it anyway.

He popped every pill into his mouth. Twenty-one by his count. Then he drank from the tap. The pills were smaller than the chunky paracetamol, but he still felt them sliding down his throat.

This isn't going to be enough.

What was he doing?

He leant against the sink.

He lurched. Felt his chest tighten. Felt his stomach grow more and more uncomfortable.

What had happened?

What had attached itself to him?

What was doing this and making him–

Stop questioning me.

"I'm sorry," he said.

He looked around. Searching for something else.

A razor sat on the edge of the bath. April's, maybe? He picked it up and turned it over.

The blade itself was stuck inside of its plastic shielding quite tightly.

"I can't get this out, it's too–"

I don't care.

Understanding it was his responsibility, he stuck his fingers inside and gripped the blade, pulling and pulling and twisting against the plastic concealment.

His fingers were bleeding quite profusely by the time he managed to get it out, but that was fine. It didn't matter. It was required pain.

"What now?" he asked.

Your wrists.

He placed the razor blade in his right hand and stuck it deep into the edge of his inside left wrist.

He stuck harder and harder, until red excretion was trembling out. Once it was deep enough, he scraped the razor blade across, his blood squirting, decorating the mirror, the toilets, the tiles, the sink.

It hurt.

Damn, it hurt.

But so what? It didn't matter. He wasn't allowed to feel it.

It's still not enough.

"What else?" Julian asked. He couldn't understand what else he would possibly need to do.

Your throat.

He lifted the razor blade to his throat.

No. Do it on your knees.

He went to his knees.

Lift your head. Reveal it all.

He raised his eyes to the ceiling, peering at the light.

He placed the razor blade on one side of his throat, stuck it in like he did with his wrist. He could feel the pressure, tightening around his gullet, pressing harder and harder against him, constricting, like a fist tightening around his oesophagus, but he didn't stop. He just kept pressing.

Once he could feel the blade all the way through his flesh, he dragged slowly and precisely, scraping through his Adam's apple and dragging to the other side of his neck.

He collapsed to the floor, the razor blade clattering against the base of the sink.

Good boy, Julian. Good boy.

His body throbbed.

His throat stung and retracted, unable to give him the air that he needed.

His eyes stayed open until the end.

He wasn't found until three hours later, when April's screams awoke the house.

WOULD YOU LIKE TWO FREE BOOKS?

Join Rick Wood's Reader's Group at www.
rickwoodwriter.com/sign-up

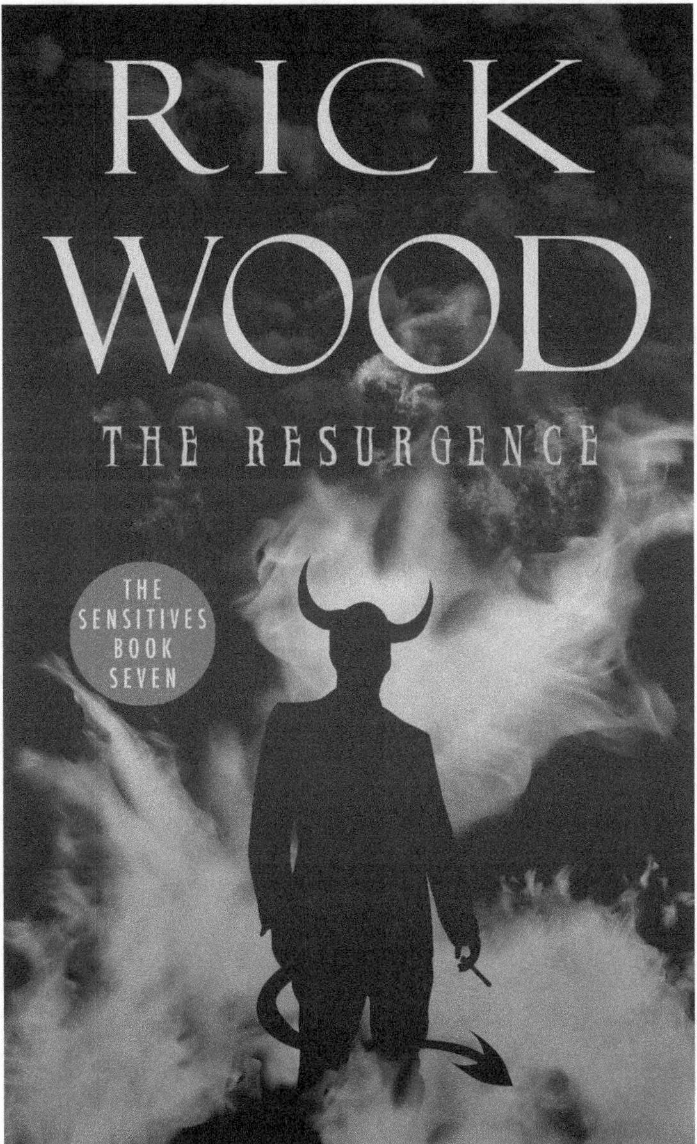
RICK
WOOD
THE RESURGENCE
THE SENSITIVES BOOK SEVEN

ALSO BY RICK WOOD

RICK
WOOD

CIA
ROSE
BOOK
ONE

AFTER
THE DEVIL
HAS WON

RICK
WOOD

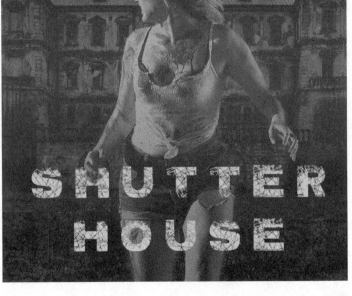

SHUTTER
HOUSE